COPY

BOOK
PRODUCTION
WAR ECONOMY
STANDARD

COPY

by

CHUS
MARTINEZ

THE STAGE

The stage is a raised structure lit by two spot lights. Beyond it there are seven rows of chairs. Behind the stage there is a wall lined with mirrors. There is no other scenery. The chairs that seat spectators during performances are reflected in the mirrors.

The ceiling of the theatre collapsed during a performance. Masonry tumbled onto the stage, and the stage machinery collapsed too.

Scattered body parts. Blood oozed over the rubble. Bodies sliced up by falling glass and crushed by tumbling masonry. Eyes pierced by rusty nails jutting from broken sections of the building's wooden frame.

Parts of bodies, hands, and feet were crushed under the rubble. Her neck was severed by a metal girder, which knocked the head two metres from her chest.

Severed limbs were thrown beyond the building, where they were consumed by rats and stray dogs.

Vermin swarmed through the rubble picking at human flesh. Entrails strewn amid blocks of concrete and shattered glass. Dead meat oozing with blood scattered throughout and beyond the wrecked theatre of the world.

Nowhere for the gaze to settle. Everything crushed or torn open. Wounds within wounds. Coldness and cruelty.

The mechanism is complex. There's a system of mirrors producing a series of reflections. Both the stage and the mirrors revolve through a number of orbits, so that it is impossible to know whether you are looking directly at the event on the stage or at a reflection, or even a reflection of a reflection.

★ ★ ★

To one side there's a rickety structure that may have been the stage, with chairs scattered around it. Seven chairs have been arranged in a semicircle. They have a plastic seat and back which is supported by a metal frame. They are all of same whitish hue, although some are slightly brighter, they are newer pieces of furniture bought to replace items that had worn out.

A man sitting on one of the chairs is reflected in a window. It is not yet dusk and so you are surprised to see such a sharp reflection when there is only low-level lighting on in the room. There are chairs scattered about, and around them plastic cups containing dregs of beer.

A semicircle of chairs is arranged in front of a structure that was once a stage, but which is now covered with piles of old newspapers and magazines. The stage floor has collapsed in the middle and old newsprint spills into it. A man is sitting in one of the chairs and his reflection fills one of the windows.

Behind the stage area the wall is lined with mirrors. The room was used as a dance studio before being rebuilt. One of the mirrors is cracked and reflects the room in altering perspectives. Also reflected in this mirror are seven people sitting on plastic chairs.

There's wall-to-wall carpeting, which has been patched together in areas where it has worn away. The furniture is mostly plastic with metal frames. There are windows cut into the walls but it is hard to see anything in the darkness outside despite the low-level lighting in the room.

There are puddles of beer on the floor with cigarette butts floating in them. Rain is dripping through holes in the ceiling, mixing with the beer. There is a rough wooden structure to one side which is made from old slats nailed together and resembles a stage.

She appears to be looking directly at you, though there's no way she can see you. Nevertheless, there are certain signs that could make her aware of your presence. Her face is lit eerily by a mirror reflecting a beam of light coming through a crack in the ceiling. The rest of her body is in shadow. She continues to stare towards you, but after a while you suspect that she's sleeping with her eyes open, in some sort of trance.

The road is covered in cracks. Some parts have been sealed off. The highway is being dismantled. Some areas are lit, some not, though this bears no relation to the road works. Sometimes it's possible to count fifty, sixty seconds of darkness, then light, then gloom again, the headlights scarcely providing any radiance, creating instead something closer to a diffuse veil constantly penetrated by the beams of the bus. Then another lit area where the cracks become visible again, the debris of the road works, piled in mounds. Then gloom.

The driver looks in his rear view mirror. The coach is occasionally lit up by street lamps, and then plunged into darkness, then light, then darkness again. Some of the passengers are looking out of a window, others are simply staring ahead.

There is a cracked pane where some teenagers threw a stone from a motorway bridge. The windscreen wipers malfunction. The bus is in semi-darkness, the passengers are silent.

The road, scarcely visible, is a series of nebulous veils repeatedly penetrated by the headlights of the bus.

Piles of debris emerge from the greyness.

There is little traffic. What there is appears initially as a diffuse glow pushing out of this substance that isn't quite darkness. The lighted areas shroud space instead of revealing it.

Lights from malls are refracted in the rain streaked windows. Distant shadows in the dimming light. The passing traffic sounds like breaking waves. Lines of traffic drawn back, then swelling forward and rushing past. The slow staccato of traffic jars against the gentle drift of distant buildings.

Shadowy forms pass behind the pointilism of raindrops, dark drifts beneath ripples of water.

No one speaks. The passengers are either looking out of the window, or staring blankly ahead. A series of reflections, and reflections of reflections, despite the low level lighting in the bus. All this superimposed over the passing landscape.

Two hands shade a section of the window, a face pressed against the pane, looking out.

Only the faintest variation of hue distinguishes the scrub of land stretching out to the horizon from the sky. It is a long time since the motorway was properly repaired, its uneven surface sends jolts through the coach. A long stretch that has been resurfaced is only intermittently lit. Deep passages engulfed in darkness, almost black, scarcely guided by the diffuse glow of the headlights, then a lit area, the darkness transformed from black to grey, then you are engulfed by the gloom again, which is somehow out of space, a sense of free-fall, awaiting the next lit area.

The illuminated areas scarcely more penetrable, they represent no more than a change of hue.

Then back to the old road with visible cracks and a steady dim light, reduced to a single lane in places where the cracks have made parts of this highway impassable.

No other vehicles. The motorway now reduced to two single lanes and the approaching glow of the boarder post, which interrupts the seemingly endless sweep of the road.

Paint flaking from walls covered in announcements for events long since passed. To one side a table with a flimsy box-like structure made from old cut offs. Towards the back, a large mirror partly reflecting the room and the windows, and a number of chairs arranged in front, still empty, though a figure can be seen in the door at the back of the room.

★　★　★

At the centre is a raised platform. The base for a statue that has not been erected. The concrete is cracked, the rain trickles through these crevices. Around the raised platform, the square is peppered with puddles. There's a strange smell – the aroma is both chemical and organic.

Water reflecting the bare branches of trees planted intermittently through the square, a grey roof of clouds behind.

Puddles all over the place. Puddles of beer, puddles of greenish water. In the puddles, junk is floating. Cigarettes, plastic cups, and broken bottles. There's a bad smell. The aroma is both chemical and organic.

The square is enclosed by buildings. At the centre is a raised plinth that once supported a fountain. To one side is a small arcade of shops.

The buildings intended to serve as retail outlets are mostly empty. Their windows gleam blankly.

Towards the back of the arcade is a store with a counter running the full length of the façade, it sells coffee. Across from the store is an empty shop. The window is cracked and dirty. Through it an empty display shelf is visible. Behind the shelf is a large mirror, and in it is a reflection of a group of teenagers sitting smoking on the plinth at the centre of the square.

There's a raised platform that was once the base of an ornamental fountain, this water feature has been removed. Teenagers are sitting on it and sparking up.

The base was originally intended as a plinth for a statue that was never erected. The unexpected success of the opposition party in a council election resulted in the politically sensitive bronze being melted down after it was sold as scrap metal.

The buildings around the square are older than the plinth and have been maintained in a better state of repair. It was constructed to replace a fountain, but now acts as a raised area where teenagers can sit and bait each other as they smoke.

To one side is a bus shelter, where a man is drinking beer. He is watching the teenagers on the raised area at the centre of the market place.

Cracked panes, with a mirror behind, now reflecting a group gathered in the bus shelter. They are drinking beer and don't appear to be waiting for a bus.

A small crowd gathers. Though barely acknowledging each other, barely lifting their heads, they are all members of an experimental theatre company who are engaged in a pre-arranged street performance.

To one side is a stage lit by two spot lights. The rest is darkness.

Fifty feet away is a hidden viewing platform. The design of the park makes the terrain difficult to navigate. There isn't a path to the viewing platform, and you are forced to switch direction in areas that are overgrown. The viewing platform is set into the side of the hill, and is easy to miss.

Among the dripping trees and barely sheltered by rain streaked leaves, a man is sitting, his head bowed down as he attempts to keep warm.

The viewing platform is covered with weeds. The concrete is cracked, ill suited to the damp climate and the harsh winter. The base is a raised semi-circle of concrete set into the slope of the hill with steps up one side. A semi-circular seating arrangement mirrors the curve of the base but with a smaller diameter. The seating is sheltered from behind and above by a wooden structure. The benches are constructed from iron and wood. The ironwork imitates the branches of a tree.

Rain drips through the holes in the roof of the seating area on the viewing platform.

Seated to one side, a man looks down at his watch and then up at the trees obscuring the view. He isn't comfortable on the rustic seating, and is steadily sinking into his coat as he attempts to stay warm.

When the park was laid out in the eighteenth-century you could gaze over the trees, across the town and down to the sea. The trees, which once framed the view, now obscure it. Their slow growth was like curtains rising very slowly at the beginning of a matinee. Now the trees themselves are the sole performers, bowing slightly in the breeze. The raised platform has become the stage and is no longer the auditorium, and the trees are the audience, and a man standing on it, slowly sinking into his coat, is a solitary actor.

The rain isn't cleansing but instead covers everything with a gelatinous skin.

It's neither warm nor cold. There is a roof of grey cloud that is almost still, made of an infinitely soft substance that will never break.

There are moments when the light changes, though without the impression of a gradual shift to new weather conditions, as if the fresh atmospheric situation had arrived instantly and yet the transition takes place without a cut or a jolt. One simply accepts that there has been a transformation.

The resort is not finished. There's a raised concrete area for an extension. It must have been set a while ago because it has already started to crack. In its current state, it resembles a stage. In some areas beach stones were pressed into the concrete when it was still wet. It's not clear if this was part of a plan that was later abandoned, or an intervention by a passer-by.

A gull hangs in the air while space shifts around it, an infinitely slow flow of phenomena swirl around the black spot of the gull's eye. The sea's surface, like gelatine, almost still, then breaking into a froth as it reaches the shore. A gull glides steadily, then stops short before dropping like a stone into the water.

There's an inner central courtyard, but where there was once a small pond, there is a hole through which one can see the collapsed masonry on the floor below.

A man is walking along the shore, dragging his feet, a dog circles around him, occasionally darting off to pull something out of the sea. The man forms a silhouette against the dimming light.

Not many people come to the resort. When the building work was abandoned, the connecting road was left uncompleted. The town is a few miles up the coast, and here there is only the resort. Occasionally teenagers descend on it bent on petty vandalism, but there are plenty of other distractions along the coast.

A man stops briefly to look at the horizon. A dog stands alert as if something might suddenly emerge from the sea; a vast shadowy form pushing out of the gelatinous surface, before plunging back down, leaving a succession of concentric circles to bear witness to the event.

Most of the rooms are empty. Much of the furniture has been scrapped or thrown into the sea.

The panelling in the foyer has been removed, exposing the plumbing and most of the cabling. Some of the plumbing has been redirected with improvised supports made up of leftovers from the panelling.

The basic structure is made of concrete, which is now badly cracked, and this conjoined with a lack of capital to rebuild it from the foundations up, is the reason the project was abandoned.

Between the main building and the sea there's a small pool. An attempt has been made to remove some of the paint, which was flaking badly, and it has been repainted in some places, though each time in a different shade of blue.

Among the rocks a crab is trying to make its way back to the sea. It seems uncertain of the direction, constantly readjusting its trajectory, pausing repeatedly to gain its bearings.

From this distance, you can scarcely see the movement of the waves. A gull glides at the same height as the cliff top, and then freezes, before dropping into the sea like a stone.

The resort isn't large. Perhaps it is only its isolated position that makes it seem like a resort rather than a family hotel. That and its sprawling lay-out.

The door to one of the rooms is propped open. The carpet has been pulled up, and half rolled in the corner, revealing the concrete floor. A table has been set in the middle. It is covered with a paper tablecloth. Around the table are plastic chairs. The table almost fills the room.

The light is dimming. It's a regional effect. The light dims after lunch, then gets steadily brighter into the evening, at which point it gets dark quite suddenly like an electric bulb being switched off.

A crab stirs and attempts to find the sea. It raises its pincers as a hand comes down and picks it up.

The grey sea endlessly sends small waves up the shore, only to draw them back again.

Dark shapes float on the surface of the water like photographic paper in a developing tray.

The sound of waves below, occasionally a gull bobbing up fixing the scene with a motionless black eye, then dropping down again.

The monument is placed on a concrete platform projecting from the cliff, supported by two iron stilts below. It is reached by descending a series of steps from the top and these are cut into the rock itself. The monument is invisible from the cliff top, and scarcely visible from the beach, where the resort is situated. The main vantage point is from out at sea. It is viewed to best advantage from passing ships.

One side of the platform is wedged into the cliff, the other three sides are closed off by an iron railing. At the centre is the monument. Or what is described as a monument. Nobody knows what it represents. The monument is a series of abstract forms. It consists of three large concrete triangles of differing widths and heights and angles. A man is standing among these triangles, but only his shoulders and head – which is turned to one side – are visible. He is looking out to sea.

Despite the general greyness, there are noticeable shifts in the clouds. They move in circles as the wind constantly changes direction. This reminds you of grease smeared on a window with a cloth.

*　　*　　*

On the floor to one side, slightly out from the wall, is a mattress. There is a window behind, and a large mirror beside this portal. The window is covered with an improvised blind.

A patch of light falls across a shoulder. The arm joined to this shoulder is still. The dome of the upper torso emerges from a general softening of detail. The rest of the body is hidden. Faint movement, a tremor of light. The arm shifts followed by the mass of the body. Posture readjusted during sleep.

The distant hum of traffic sounds like waves breaking on a beach.

A hand brushes over the covers, the arm follows, both settle in a hollow just beneath the mound of the body. The head shifts into the patch of light. A makeshift blind billows. The light illuminates her head, which is turned towards him, her face obscured by hair.

The window is open just a crack. A blind made from a sheet pinned to the window frame billows, and as it does so a rectangle of light expands and contracts, illuminating an arm, a shoulder, a head.

There is a faint stirring, breath is exhaled, then inhaled and exhaled again. The body is shifting under the blankets, almost imperceptibly with the movement being audible rather than visible.

The rest of the room is in darkness, a kind of diffuseness in which forms suggest themselves, and then withdraw. The gleam of a mirror, objects scattered over the table, the mattress on the floor, the sleeping body, the faintest stirring of breath, and occasionally minor body movements, mild disturbance in the calm of sleep.

An eye constructs forms in the ebbing darkness. A table with a mirror leaning on it, the mattress on the floor. A patch of light now illuminating a pale hand and wrist. An arm, only vaguely suggested against the paler shade of the blanket. The occasional billowing of the sheet pinned in front of the open window.

Elsewhere there are similar rooms, and yet others identical to it. Newspaper covers the window. A table is set up for a game of cards.

A man a standing among piles of booklets. In another place, the piles have become mounds. The stacks create a warren of streets in the workshop.

To one side a wooden structure is covered in newspapers and magazines, books and pamphlets. The drip-drip of the rain outside, audible rather than visible, hidden by a blind pinned over the window. On the wooden structure, among the stacks of booklets, is a puppet theatre made of old off-cuts from an earlier puppet theatre. The puppet theatre is still under construction.

Arranged in front of the puppet theatre are several rows of chairs. Plastic seats and backs with a metal frame. The same whitish hue, though some slightly brighter than others, newer furniture bought to replace items that had worn out.

There's wall-to-wall carpeting, which has been patched together in areas where it has worn away. The furniture is mostly plastic with metal frames, bought in stages to replace items that were worn out. There are windows cut into the walls, but it is hard to see anything in the gloom beyond the window despite the low-level of lighting in the room.

There's an old wooden structure made from slats. Off-cuts and pieces dismantled from the main structure of the building. The building is slowly collapsing and a new structure is emerging from within. We pay you to play. Even if you have no erection problems! Enlarge your penis with our magic pills! It's as easy as 1, 2, 3!

The coast is covered in stones. A group has gathered around a car that crossed the barrier and crashed down onto the rocky shore below.

One passenger was thrown some distance by the impact.

A crowd has assembled around the accident.

The string puppets are only capable of rudimentary movements. The theatre is dismantled after each performance. It is stored alongside the puppets in a room at the back of the theatre. Props belonging to various theatres companies are stored together and can be assembled in various combinations to meet the specific requirements of each performance.

The puppet theatre consists of a miniature stage and auditorium. Due of the limited scale of the production, the audience is represented by six puppets sitting with their backs to the real audience.

No one has bothered to keep track of the newspaper articles that served as the starting point for the performances. Some of the scripts have been preserved, but these largely consist of instructions to the puppeteers, and it's not always easy to reconstruct the narrative.

It's raining and you have a long trek ahead of you. Stopping at an internet café to check your email you feel the first twinges of a migraine. You know you shouldn't be drinking coffee but instead of wasting the beverage you take an aspirin with it. The combination of coffee and medicine tastes unpleasant. The internet café is cramped. You don't have any email, and this leaves you feeling deflated. You want to go home and get into bed. You can use the migraine as an excuse.

Rubbish is turning to mush in the rain.

You want to sit down. You follow the man walking purposefully down the street. You find yourself in a neighbourhood whose sidewalks thrum with pedestrians. A market square. In the middle, there's a raised platform where some teenagers are sitting. The shops are mostly closed. In a roofed arcade to one side there is a store selling coffee. You stand at the counter drinking coffee from a plastic cup.

You stop and look into a shop window. The shop is empty and all the displays have been removed. Behind the display case is a mirror. You catch a glimpse of your reflection.

You see a group gathered in a bus stop behind you. One of them is pointing, but you cannot see where.

You make your way past rubbish that is turning to mush in the rain.

You walk on and reach an estuary. You have forgotten why you came here.

The pulsing in your head is now more regular than when the migraine came on. You find this reassuring.

You go back to the café you just passed. You buy a coffee to go and sit in the square, despite the drizzle. On the raised area, two teenagers are having a mock fight, which is turning nasty.

You catch a glimpse of your face in a shop window and are surprised by the blankness of your expression.

Trees, dripping wet, emerge from the greyness.

Streets piled with rubbish. Streets within streets.

You turn and go into the café. There are puddles of beer on the floor with cigarette butts floating in them. There's the perpetual rain dripping through holes in the ceiling, mixing with the beer. There's a rough wooden structure to one side made from old slats nailed together resembling a stage.

Apart from you, there's only one other customer sitting at the bar. The waitress is standing silently beside him. Behind the bar is a large mirror, which reflects the sea through the open window. A gull hovers in the sky.

You sit down at a table and clear a space amongst the debris of plastic cups. You sip coffee and ponder whether or not to tip the waitress who brought it to you.

On the beach a group of teenagers are trying to dismantle a car that was dumped there. The sea is greasy. The shore is covered in large rocks and stones.

Performances are developed collaboratively through improvisation. They are usually based on news events that are of interest to the local community. This process has never been explicitly discussed, but the procedure is so well established that it would be difficult to change it.

The scenery is often adapted from photographs cut out of newspapers. Blown up photocopies, painted backdrops and three dimensional reconstructions have all been used.

The company stages plays in schools and public halls. Before each performance, the local area is fly-posted to publicise the event.

*　*　*

Puddles all over the place. Puddles of beer, puddles of greenish water. In the puddles, junk is floating. Cigarettes, plastic cups, and broken bottles. There's a bad smell. The aroma is both chemical and organic.

The discussion is drifting despite the urgent necessity for a collective decision. There are two factions and each is too entrenched to reach an agreement.

The wall-to-wall carpeting has been patched together in areas where it has worn away. The chairs are plastic with metal frames. Although identical in design, they vary in hue depending on the extent of their exposure to dirt and light. There are windows cut into the walls, but it is hard to see anything in the darkness outside despite the low-level lighting in the room.

You look up for a moment, then down again at your notebook.

There's a table, now placed in the middle of the room with chairs set around it. The chairs are plastic with metal frames. All of a whitish hue, though some slightly lighter, these are newer furnishings bought to replace items that had worn out.

A man is sitting on one of the chairs. His reflection is visible in the window. This surprises you because it is not yet dusk and there is only low level lighting in the room. There are chairs scattered about, and around them plastic cups containing dregs of beer.

Far off, you can hear the sea, a gull.

There are puddles of beer on the floor with cigarette butts floating in them. There's the perpetual rain dripping through holes in the ceiling, mixing with the beer. There's a rough wooden structure to one side made from old slats nailed together which resembles a stage.

In the middle of the room is a large table. Most of those present are either gazing down at the table they're gathered around or else are staring blankly ahead. Several notebooks lie open on the blue table with pens beside them.

A woman brings coffee. Some old cups are cleared away. These meetings take place on a regular basis. The company is convinced the discussion is drawing to a conclusion, although one faction hasn't grasped where the argument is going. Most of the collective believe everything has already been said but since nature abhors a vacuum, time first buckled, then bent, and has now reversed itself. Living in the shadow of silent majorities and having been born in the 1980s, you make a point of having nothing more to say. The discussion is moribund.

The meeting is punctuated by long pauses in which the group scrutinises itself and stares stubbornly at the yellow table. Words from an eighteenth-century novel that started a suicide cult spring into your mind. No longer under the reign of will and representation, the group knows very little about the philosoph-

24

ical sources from which aesthetic theory was constructed and instead approaches the many problems it encounters from the perspective of Freud and diagnosis. Someone is keeping notes. During the pauses, the minute taker looks up to see whether the discussion is going to continue. You stare blankly at him then fix your gaze on the bright red table.

There is a pulsing in your head. You are having difficulty concentrating. You have stopped taking notes. You know further discussion is pointless. You visualise the argument as being red with purple flashes.

Three speakers dominate the proceedings. Each makes the same point, over and over and over again. A recalcitrant majority remain stubbornly silent. They are not convinced by the fine phrases they keep hearing. Those speaking attempt to second guess the positions of the silent majority, but continually return to the same theme, since they are incapable of formulating an argument that runs counter to their own.

There is a pause. Someone stands up and goes to the window

The brown table is moved to the centre of the room. There is the screech of chairs on the floor as they are shifted. A man brings in beer, old cups are cleared away. The meetings take place on a regular basis, but all the company members have other responsibilities, and fixing times to meet always entails compromise. For the silent majority in the group, the outcome of the meeting is a foregone conclusion, and there's little point in further discussion. The founders of the theatre company optimistically believed that its activities and influence would continuously expand. That said the collective is now imploding in a subdued fashion, like a slow motion reversal of an explosion or some other catastrophe. The group is absorbing all the energy it has generated over the years and neutralising it.

Every half hour there's a long drawn out sound, a low droning. You visualise it as being green with purple flashes. It is scarcely audible. Some of the group look up, uncertain as to whether they actually heard anything at all. Dogs bark.

You try to keep notes, partly as a way of remaining attentive to what is being said, although you feel that the same point is being made again and again. However, there are always slight differences in the way this matter is formulated and minor changes of tone. These variations aren't always evident in your notes. Your written record keeps shifting as you attempt to summarise the same old argument in new ways. You imagine the notes you are making being played in the key of G, and you visualise them as deep space; black with flashes of darker blackness.

Far off the sound of the sea, a gull.

For some time, you sit staring at your notepad. You look up. Some of the group are now standing at the window, looking out through the panes stained by rain and dirt. The grey sky and the trees beyond. The fading light.

Far off there is a strange sound. It is difficult to distinguish it from other noises. The sea, a gull, the sound of dogs barking, the traffic, an electric storm. It could be the reverberation of bells, where each tone has lost its distinct shape and merges imperceptibly with the others. A single extended note as if coming from the some eldritch dimension unknown to man, not a human sound, but a slow shattering echo without beginning or end. You don't know when this ricochet effect kicked in, and I suspect you'll be dead before it ends. The dim hush is pornographic, its obscenity lies in the fact that it can't be visualised.

There has been talk about putting a booklet together. It would lay out the issues that have been raised in recent meetings. No longer under the reign of will and representation, the group knows very little about the philosophical sources from which aesthetic theory was constructed and instead approaches the many problems it encounters from the perspective of Freud and diagnosis. A company member has a cousin who runs a printing workshop. The pamphlet would be printed in a short run on paper plates and sold at performances.

You stand up and move to the window. Outside the same greying light filtered by the branches of a tree.

There have been several discussions about the function of the puppet theatre. Its themes are topical but the children who participate in the shows remain unaware of this. The performances always contain scenes of Sadean cruelty. The company believes this provides an outlet for childish fears and it is intended to have a cathartic effect. One of the founders of the company wrote their undergraduate dissertation on Wilhelm Reich, another made a study of Peter Brooke's *Marat/Sade*.

The puppets representing the audience are only supposed to be operated in crucial scenes. At the beginning of the play there is a vignette in which a member of the audience tries to stand up and climb onto the stage (he is restrained by two other members of the audience), and these puppets appear again in the scene where the auditorium roof collapses.

The kinder operate the puppets using strings. They stand on a raised platform behind the stage. Not all les enfants operate the puppets at any one time, although those bambini not involved often become impatient and push at the children operating the mannequins, so that they can make use of free dolls. As a result the stage becomes crowded with players and their threads get tangled.

★   ★   ★

An hour's drive from the city there is a town by the sea. The motorway follows the estuary. You take a bus, passing through the suburbs. Outside it's raining. Though it's only the early afternoon, it is already dark. The lights of shopping malls pierce the blackness engulfing the slow flow of traffic from the city.

The motorway is in a poor state of repair and is frequently reduced to one lane by road works. The world is imploding in a subdued fashion, like a slow motion reversal of an explosion or some other catastrophe. The best lack all conviction, the worst are filled with a passionate intensity.

You take the bus to a small town by the sea with your colleagues from the puppet theatre. They are not talking. They seem unaware of your presence, their attention is elsewhere. Some are looking out of the side windows, and some are staring straight ahead into space. Blackness. The void. Too many light-years between stars. You imagine yourself to be in suspended animation. Nature abhors a vacuum; time buckled, bent, reversed but never regained. The group is absorbing all the energy it has generated over the years and neutralising it. The resultant dim hush is pornographic, its obscenity lies in the fact that it can't be visualised.

You pass piles of rubbish. The artistic director of your company worships waste; she claims to be drawing on Bataille's theory of solar economics. If nature abhors a vacuum then it must be a social construction, there is nothing at all in deep space.

You are already regretting your decision to make this trip. The recent meetings have been tiresome. There was a major bust up, and now it feels as if you are living in what Thomas Hobbes claimed was the natural state of mankind, a war of all against all.

You use your hands to shade a section of the window and look out.

There is only the faintest variation in the hue that distinguishes the scrub of land stretching out to the horizon from the sky. The motorway is in a poor state of repair and its uneven surface sends jolts through the coach. There are long smooth stretches of road with only intermittent lighting. You are engulfed in shadows, the world around you is pitch black, only the diffuse glow of headlights offer any respite from this gloom; then a lit area before you are plunged back into a dark night of the soul. You imagine yourself to be in free fall; fear and trembling. You look for colours out of space in anticipation of the next lit area.

Darkness, light, darkness, light. Darkness.... light.... darkness.... light.... Darkness, light, darkness, light. Darkness. Light. Darkness. Light. Darkness, light, darkness, light. Darkness.... light.... darkness.... light.... Darkness. Light. Darkness. Light. Darkness, light, darkness, light. Darkness.... light.... darkness.... light.... Darkness, light, darkness, light. Darkness. Light. Darkness. Light. Darkness, light, darkness, light. Darkness.... light.... darkness.... light.... Darkness. Light. Darkness. Light.

Back to the old road with its cracks visible in a steady dim light. Reduced to a single lane where surface disintegration has made the road impassable. The highway is imploding in a subdued fashion, like a slow motion reversal of an explosion or some other catastrophe that drags on forever.

The tinted windows create the impression that it is evening although it's only early afternoon. Dim lights pierce the darkness, and are refracted by the water trickling down the windowpanes. Space is deep.

All the seats are upholstered with the same patterned material. It's a variation on a check, and in this deviation the squares have started to drift away from what Euclid would have considered their proper place. These coverings make you think of dying planets sucked into long dead stars, black dwarfs, white dwarfs, and entropy in deep space.

You are crossing the suburbs, watching shopping malls pass like spaceships in the night sky, clouds across the moon, shadows at dusk. Love without sound. Here come the fleas.

A company member has a cousin who runs a printing workshop. The booklet will be ready in a week. The collective is pleased with the design. It was one of the few things they could agree upon in recent meetings.

The pamphlet design is plain and clear, visually you have always favoured bold lines and noble simplicity, so this pleases you. That said you would like to cut much of the text. You'd wanted to make a clear statement but the collective insisted on adding caveats and unneeded clarifications until these dense thickets of rhetoric grew inexorably into an impenetrable jungle of words that overran the entire manifesto. From your point of view what was important was to create an immediate impact; but instead you've ended up mirroring the slow drift of an ice flow, the imperceptible passage of distant galaxies through hyper space. The collective is imploding in a subdued fashion, like a slow motion reversal of an explosion or some other catastrophe.

Puddles all over the place. Puddles of beer, puddles of greenish water. In the puddles, junk is floating. Cigarettes, plastic cups, and broken bottles. There's a bad smell. The aroma is both chemical and organic.

The sense of elation produced by the publication of the pamphlet lasted for weeks. The collective briefly regained a sense of unity and the recalcitrant majority weren't at all concerned by the ways in which the manifesto misrepresented their activities. The coldness of deep space thousands of degrees below freezing.

A month later there was a discussion that degenerated into a row. The collective, who were elated by the success they believed was bound to follow on from the publication of their pamphlet, are now at war with each other. The puppets representing the collective are only supposed to be operated in crucial scenes. At the beginning of the play there is a vignette in which the artistic director tries to stand up and climb onto the stage to assault an actor who has fluffed his lines, but she is restrained by puppets representing two male actors.

The stage is a raised platform with a proscenium arch and a real curtain. The backdrop is a large mirror reflecting the faces of the puppet audience, and the real audience behind. Most of the action takes place on the stage within the stage until the roof collapses over the auditorium, then the main drama switches to the audience, with the actors on stage becoming the spectators. The brutality of this violent scene serves to underscore the mixture of farce and sentimentality which characterise the overall tone of the play.

Behind the puppet theatre, and to one side, three children provide musical accompaniment. The tallest plays a keyboard, the smallest the triangle, and the third a xylophone.

The use of direct speech is avoided. The children refused to write dialogue. Speech is suggested by the use of music – which implies the tone rather than the sense of these silent exchanges. There are a number of scenes where the gestures of the puppets, the mise-en-scene and the musical accompaniment prove insufficient to generate any definite meaning. At these points the puppets in their opaque nothingness literally become "the ill-will of the people", the spongy referent that animates all post-democratic societies. The cold of interstellar space thousands of degrees below freezing.

You pick her up in your car. The windscreen is cracked from a stone that some teenagers threw from a motorway bridge. The windscreen wipers are faulty and it is raining. Behold a pale horse.

You drive slowly. You can only see a few feet beyond the car in the gluey fog. A child was killed on this road, its ghost allegedly appears at night seeking out hit and run drivers.

She doesn't speak. You are surprised she doesn't want to talk about the row at the puppet theatre. The dim hush is pornographic, its obscenity lies in the fact that it can't be visualised.

You are late. The collective sits around a pale pink table in a room with wall-to-wall carpeting. They were waiting for you to arrive before beginning the meeting, but you assumed they were running late.

The ocean is a neutral grey. The sky is a few shades lighter. Some children are trying to pull a log out of the sea.

You go for a stroll. The rocks are green and slippery. As you walk, you brush against their damp surfaces. You take off your shoes and feel brown mud oozing between your toes. A hundred meters from the resort is a hut. Its greenish hue matches the rocks, the stone of the cliff face, the brown and green mud.

The floor of the hut is made of stones brought up from the beach. It is easy to trip on the uneven surface.

Stones from the beach were set in the wet concrete. The floor was laid in sections. Each part is slightly different from those that preceded it. A uniform surface could only be created by starting again from scratch.

Debris from the dismantled floor rolled up in a carpet. The materials for a new floor block the door. Reconstruction work cannot begin until the room is cleared.

The puppets are strewn over the stage, threads hanging limply over them. A long mournful chord comes from the keyboard as the theatre is plunged into darkness. Then the lights come up and the puppeteers move to the front of the stage to bow and bask in the applause.

The town centre is run down. One or two shops appear promising, but they stock the same junk as everywhere else. After an hour you have only made two purchases and you need to stock up on supplies.

For a while the discussion went well. Most of the group considered it productive. Then a sense of semantic confusion set in, with the opposed factions taking the same terms to mean quite different things. And as for the majority of the collective who in their abstract emptiness stood in so well for that spongy referent "the masses", they grew ever more silent and ever more recalcitrant. The slow drift of ice flows. The dim hush of pornography. The cruelty of deep space.

On the street a group assembles. They are standing in a semi-circle. Is it a queue, or something more sinister? Bon-Euclidean geometries. Voices green, purple and red. Strange folds in the fabric of time and space. The universe buckled, bent and went into reverse. Apocalypse postponed, time running backwards and in slow-mo.

*   *   *

You leave the flat to get some air. You have felt unsettled since waking up. Your nerves are frayed. Your stomach aches and the pain is spreading through your limbs. The pounding of your blood sends tremors through your body. You have developed an allergy to alcohol.

You walk along the canal and down to the estuary. The sky is leaden, despite a strange glow that emanates from the clouds. Colours out of space. The light and your movement have a calming effect, but when you stop and rest you are overwhelmed by feelings of existential dread and can't bear to look at the water.

You want to follow the estuary down to sea wall, but it's still some way off and you are tired. There are shops selling bread and canned vegetables and beer. Sometimes there's a place to sit and drink coffee, but your stomach refuses to hold down anything stronger than water.

It starts to drizzle. You passed the last store some time ago. The sky suddenly darkens, though far off there is a pale yellowish glow that might be the fading sun or the light from a shipyard. You can see cranes creaking and although muffled by the drizzle, you think you can hear the sound of gravel being poured into shipping containers. Simultaneously the darkness envelops you in an obscene silence, where isolated sounds reach you as if from a long dead world.

A stray dog looms up in the darkness. Its grey pelt resembles the grey of the brick, the grey concrete, the grey sky. It stops in front of you, oblivious of your presence, and starts to clean its paws.

You walk towards the stray. The dog looks up and fixes you with an unblinking stare. As you move closer, it remains entirely still, unblinking. It could be stuffed. But then, it looked up, turns its head away, and continues cleaning its paws.

One of the cranes is moving. It is a dark shadow against the sky now scarcely lighter. Gleams of light pick out parts of the drizzle. The intermittent creaking sound you hear might be a crane or strange shifts in the air itself.

Gulls swoop and glide low over the estuary, catch a pocket of air and are lifted up again to hover and wait before swooping again, they are paler than the sky, their black eyes watching the blank surface of the water. Waiting for the surface to break and then swooping.

Far off there is a strange sound. It is difficult to distinguish it from other noises. The sea, a gull, pouring gravel, the creaking cranes, the sound of dogs barking, the traffic, an electric storm. It could be the reverberation of bells, where each tone has lost its distinct shape and merges imperceptibly with the others. A single extended note as if coming from the some eldritch dimension unknown to man, not a human sound, but a slow shattering echo without beginning or end. You don't know when this ricochet effect kicked in, and I suspect you'll be dead before it ends. The dim hush is pornographic, its obscenity lies in the fact that it can't be visualised.

★   ★   ★

Six people are seated around a plastic table placed in front of a bar, they are drinking beer and playing cards. They have oil stains on their hands. The bar is the only thing lit up apart from the occasional streetlamp. Most of the houses have been abandoned. The shipyard is no longer operating.

A man stands up. Lays down his last card and leaves.

You sit down on an empty chair. The seating is arranged in a semi-circle around the table. The bar behind you has an open window through which the barman passes the beer. Opposite the bar is a high brick wall with shards from broken bottles set into concrete at the top. Above the wall you can see a few of the cranes that were once used to unload the barges or cargo ships.

An awning protects drinkers sitting on the street outside a bar from drizzle but not from the cold. The drizzle is reaching the level of dispersion at which it becomes mist.

There is a brick wall topped by shards of glass, covered in tatters of old posters, now illegible, the silhouettes of cranes, the occasional gull bobbing up above the horizon of the wall before dropping down, the drizzle is turning to mist. These elements fade in and out of visibility depending on the level of light and the density of mist.

A hand lays a card on the table. A man leaves.

A general clatter comes from behind the theatre, the puppeteers are preparing for the start of their show.

As the curtain rises, a puppet is standing at the front of the stage to announce the beginning of the performance. A slow crescendo comes from a keyboard accompanied by a repeated sequence of notes on a xylophone. The puppet audience clap. Some of them stand up. The puppeteers are in trouble. Some of the puppet threads are tangled. The curtain comes down.

Though, there's a specific narrative underlying the sequence of events on the stage, some aspects inevitably get lost. This is partly due to the lack of explicatory dialogue, but mostly because the puppets cannot convey much emotional subtlety either in their faces or their gestures.

A month ago it was decided that new lights should be installed in the booth at the back of the theatre, and since then the old ones have been dangling from old cables that are half wrenched out.

You are laying a few cables for an intercom unit. A number of shafts are already installed in the wall, so all you need to do is thread the new cables through.

The cabling is tangled. Most of the work is just straightening it out. About sixty percent of the wiring is redundant and can be scrapped. The rest needs to be refitted.

You pass heaps of rubbish, now turning to mush in the rain. Streets within streets.

You are still tired, but the pulsing in your head has quietened down, which puts you more at ease. Outside, there is a strange glow in the sky. It is distinct from the grey roof of cloud.

You reach the market place. There is an electronics shop on the corner. On the raised platform at the centre of the square, a group of teenagers are having a mock fight that is turning nasty. A man sitting in the bus shelter wants to intervene, but other people hold him back.

The electronics shop is closed, but the sign on its door still advertises it as open. You bang repeatedly. No reply.

You search for somewhere to sit down. You walk past an empty shop and catch your reflection in a mirror. In the arcade, you find a concession selling coffee. You stand at the counter drinking from a plastic cup.

You bang on the door. Eventually a light comes on. The shop assistant opens the grill and then the door.

The shop is chaotic. Everything heaped up. The cable is in the basement. You only need a few short strips. You ask for a detector to track movement through the theatre. The assistant starts rummaging around. Eventually the assistant finds a suitable unit. You think of dying planets sucked into long dead stars, black dwarfs, white dwarfs, and entropy in deep space.

You follow the canal to the theatre. Gulls gather and disperse against the grey sky.

You join a number of lengths of cable and thread them along shafts above the false ceiling in the foyer. You drill holes for the detector unit.

You thread cables through shafts already holding other cables.

You fit an intercom unit to the booth at the back of the theatre, which is sealed off from the rest of the auditorium by a viewing window.

You connect a camera to the intercom unit at the door, and also to the foyer, and the auditorium. The building is riddled with holes and so it's not difficult to rig up the cable. There's also an old detector unit that needs to be checked. It is defective. The slow drift of distant galaxies through hyper space.

★   ★   ★

You wander up a dark hill. At the top there's a viewing platform. A black terrier circles around you, trailing a lead. The dim hush is pornographic, its obscenity lies in the fact that it can't be visualised.

As you climb further up the hill, the trees start to thicken so that only patches of grey sky appear among the branches. It smells very damp. You can't find the viewing platform. The coldness of deep space thousands of degrees below freezing.

As you look up, patches of grey move almost imperceptibly in the gloom. Anti-colours from inner space. Are you looking for the cheapest software? We have the software you want dirt cheap.

Patches of grey darken behind the leaflets branches. There is a curious glow in the air, which illuminates objects from within, so that night never really arrives, and as the sun goes down a graininess takes hold, its vibrations producing the peculiar illumination.

The viewing platform is covered with weeds. The concrete is cracked, ill suited to the damp climate and the harsh winter. The base is a raised semi-circle of concrete set into the slope of the hill with steps up one side. A semi-circular seating arrangement mirrors the curve of the base but with a smaller diameter. The seating is sheltered from behind and above by a wooden structure. The benches are constructed from iron and wood. The ironwork imitates the branches of a tree.

A man climbs up onto the viewing platform with a small dog circling around him.

The throbbing in your head is more regular, which for puts you at ease. You look down at your watch. There's a bad smell. The aroma is both chemical and organic.

Grey trees, dripping wet. Make her buckle and moan all night when you split that pussy wide open.

The trees obscure the view that the platform was sited to exploit. Gleams of light penetrate the mesh of branches. The trees resemble actors or dancers, the branches shifting slightly. Perhaps, the raised platform is a stage, and the trees are the audience. You are a solitary actor on a stage that consists of the entire world.

You feel tired. You sit down, your thoughts drift. Strange folds in the fabric of time and space. Viagra at $1.41 per dose! Best online drug store! Our purpose is to provide PC and Macintosh software and computer solutions at the lowest prices available. Cyberspace is anti-matter, sucking in human subjectivity. The theatre of the world implodes in a slow motion reversal of an explosion or some other catastrophe. The web is absorbing all the energy consumer society has generated over the years and neutralising it.

After the theatre collapsed, the seats and stage machinery were removed. Nevertheless, the damaged structure still resembled a stage. An attempt was made to seal off the theatre, but the building was so riddled with holes that vagrants and gangs of juvenile delinquents inevitably strayed in.

You are late. The collective were waiting for you to arrive before beginning the meeting, but you assumed they were running late.

You think of the conference held in this theatre a year ago. You weren't really interested at the time. There were a series of power cuts. The conference ended in fading natural light, without amplification, in shambles.

The stage is a raised structure lit by two spot lights. Then seven rows of chairs. Behind the stage, there is a wall lined with mirrors. No other scenery. The mirrors reflect the empty chairs of the auditorium.

On both sides of the stage actors wait in groups, aware that though they are part of the audience, they are also part of the performance.

There is an outline of the play but no finished script. The synopsis is fragmented and reads like a description of a performance by an amateur journalist with no knowledge of theatre conventions.

The auditorium is empty aside from the director and a few assistants. The stage is lit by two spots and there is also illumination from the windows. The theatre space is a large hall used for rehearsals, meetings and small conferences. There are some additional rooms and a foyer.

The theatre is in a poor state of repair. Yesterday the lighting rig collapsed. The debris has been heaped up at the side of the stage. Cables still hang loosely from the ceiling.

There is a stage with a lighting rig above it. The lights have been removed but old cables still hang down from the ceiling. Two spot lights still function and provide patches of illumination on the stage.

From the back of the hall it's difficult to make out what's happening on stage. The lighting rig is broken and the only illumination is dim grey daylight seeping through the windows under the roof.

The stage has been cleared by pushing the props and scenery to one side. The lighting is broken, but some natural light filters in through the upper windows. The entire cast is present but since the piece is still being developed only a few of them have any direct role in today's proceedings. The others are there to observe and to think about what they might contribute as the improvisations develop into something resembling a play.

There is no script and the synopsis you have is fragmented and reads like a description of a performance by an amateur journalist with no knowledge of theatre conventions.

You arrive late. The actors are on the stage but the rehearsal hasn't started. You are unsure about whether you actually want to participate in this production. There have been endless disagreements about the future of the group. Initial discussions about this new piece were euphoric, but all enthusiasm evaporated when it became apparent that none of the younger actors and actresses was prepared to appear nude. You sided with the older cast members and artistic director who told the juniors they were theatrical dilettantes.

The stage is littered with scenery from another production. To one side is a mattress on the floor. At the back is a table of indeterminate colour, in the half-light it looks brown but you suspect it is actually red. Hey Goddess of Spam! At Green Meanie, we will PAY YOU to view websites, complete offers, sample products, signup for free trials, play games, shop online, and more! There is currently over $2,000 available in offer earnings! Join now to receive a $0.10 sign-up bonus!

You've felt unsettled since waking up. Your nerves are frayed. Your stomach aches and the pain is spreading through your limbs. The pounding of your blood sends tremors through your body. You have developed an allergy to milk.

Several actors have conferred with you about forming a rival theatre company. Colours out of space, over 8000 styles of genuine Swiss replica watch.

From the back of the hall it's difficult to make out what's happening on stage. Props have been heaped up in the wings. Three actors stand beneath the spot lights waiting for the rehearsal to begin. Coldness and cruelty. Dark planets revolving around a dying sun. Enlarge your penis with our magic pills! It's as easy as 1, 2, 3! If you have a cell phone we've got a guaranteed prize for you!

You are called forward. You walk up to the stage. The director asks how you feel about what you're doing. Without much conviction you reply: "Acting adds zest to my life." The director rephrases your words telling you to write down and repeat: "The acting trip is a groove sensation." You sound far more convincing mouthing this hot little catch-phrase and you start to believe it.

You watch a series of improvisations from the side of the stage. Mail Scanner has detected a possible fraud attempt! King style for Dorothea, enormous phallus for Eva, king-size cock for Dorothea!

You move to the front of the stage. You turn to face another actor. She looks at you and you have no idea what you should say to her. You say the first thing that comes into your head: "You have that unique look movie producers seek out. I'm always looking out for talent. You have a great personality and attitude."

The stage is filled with the props from another production. There's an elaborate system of mirrors on movable frames.

She seems to be looking directly at you, though there's no way she can see you. Nevertheless she could be aware of your presence. Her face is lit by a mirror reflecting a beam of light coming through a crack in the ceiling. The rest of her body is in shadow. She stares towards you, but you suspect that she's asleep with her eyes open in a cataleptic trance.

The director tells you to stop your improvisation. You inscribe what she says in a notebook, before reading back: "You're hot babe, you got it king style!"

The cast are engaged in a game from which everybody else is excluded, the actors ignore the stage hands and other auxiliaries gathered in the auditorium, and behave as if this support team is merely present by chance.

The director wants the actors to wear their own clothes and to speak with their own voices. Their words shouldn't be addressed to the audience, or even to each other, but to themselves. She wants to avoid a single scene, and instead have several scenes that occur simultaneously in the style of a 1960s art 'happening'.

The light scarcely changes in this smallish room. Always the same leaden grey. There's a window with old newspaper stuck over it. Are you looking for the cheapest software? We have the software you want dirt cheap.

Doors on either side of the stage allow the actors to enter and exit. For the rehearsal, however, the actors who are not directly involved in the scene often wait in the shadowy area at the side of the stage, or else climb down from this elevation to watch from the auditorium. The director has stated that he wants the actors to have a sense of the whole production and to become familiar with the acting styles of their cohorts. According to the director, the actors should use their normal gestures and speaking voice, but be conscious of how this is only one element among many. He works closely on the rhythm and phrasing of gestures and words, by focussing on the specific breathing patterns of each performer. If a word in falls outside their natural breathing cycle, then there should be a pause while they take a breath, followed by the final word or words of each sentence, irrespective of its effect on syntax.

On both sides of the stage, the actors wait in groups. Viagra at $1.41 per dose! Best online drug store! Our purpose is to provide PC and Macintosh software and computer solutions at the lowest prices available.

The spot lights go out. The only illumination comes from the windows under the roof. For a moment there is silence. Only the drip-drip of the rain on the windows and roof. The director stops an actress and suggests she changes her lines. The thespian writes the new formulation in her notebook before repeating what she has written.

A dog climbs up onto the stage. It pauses stage-centre looking out into the auditorium, then continues to stage-right and lies down. It pricks up its ears, remains alert for a while, though without getting up. Then settles.

There is a droning sound that makes the windows tremble slightly. The dog pricks up its ears, settles down again.

There's graffiti sprayed over the mirrors and the stage is littered with bottles and cans, partly swept up. There is also an old mattress on the stage and a few chairs.

The dog gets up from where it has been lying and starts sniffing around the cans and empty bottles. A woman gets up from the mattress, goes over to the dog and strokes it.

Her dress pulled tight over her back, you can see her spine and ribs.

To one side, there's a raised platform, operating like a stage within a stage. There's a scene where the roof collapses on a theatre.

You are tired, but the director wants to continue. He wants to work on your breathing. He doesn't want to use a script, but some of the actors are taking notes. The actors have been instructed to learn sequences of movement that over time become routine. Words are threaded through these martial art like patterns. There is an outline of the play but no finished script. The synopsis is fragmented and reads like a description of a performance by an amateur journalist with no knowledge of theatre conventions. There are no coherent scenes but instead a series of activities that run simultaneously. The actors wear their own clothes, speak with their own voices, use their own everyday gestures. At the moment the lighting is limited to two spots that occasionally go out so that the only illumination comes from the windows under the roof.

You walk over to the mirror at the back of the stage. The building was once used as a dance studio. The mirror is scratched and cracked in places. It has been sprayed with graffiti: "Ed wuz 'ere 13 October 2008." Underneath in a different had but the same pink paint: "Death Lives, Oedipus Wrecks!" You catch a glimpse of yourself in the mirror. Your body is illuminated by the spot light overhead. Mail Scanner has detected a possible fraud attempt!

You go to her flat when she's out. You are surprised by the disorder. The kitchen's grimy. You find some cigarettes in a drawer.

You root around for an ashtray. You pick up some books and just as quickly discard them. In the middle of the room there's a table with splayed legs. The table is reflected in a large mirror next to the door.

There are two posters pinned to the wall. One has a lot of text. It's information about a conference that took place in an old theatre. You didn't go to the conference. The other poster is larger and pinned a little higher. There's a photograph of a woman standing by a window and looking out at some trees. It's black and white. A film poster.

You go to the table. There's a notebook that you've seen elsewhere. You flick through it trying to find the point where the writing breaks off.

There's a square in front of the apartment with a raised platform, which could be used for dances, though it's covered in leaves. A child has climbed up, and is busy scraping wet leaves around with his right foot. There's a little dog straying about.

You feel hungry. There is nothing you'd eat in the food cupboard. On the floor there's a plastic bag with some tinned soup. You try to open the can with a knife.

You have pamphlets to pick up from the printer's. When you arrive, the printer is out to lunch. His assistant isn't sure where your booklets are. You have to wait. You sit down and watch the assistant adjusting the registration on an off-set litho machine.

Hard to know how anybody could work in such chaos. Over 8000 styles of genuine Swiss replica watch.

★ ★ ★

To dramatise the scene where the roof collapses over the auditorium of the theatre, slides of real destruction are projected onto the back of the theatre, which, because of the mirror behind the stage, is then partially reflected back into the space where the real audience are sitting. The slides are mostly taken from newspaper articles about recent wars, mixed in are a few archive photographs.

Images of carnage projected over the audience. The slow drift of distant galaxies through hyper space.

★ ★ ★

The light in the room never changes. Always the same leaden grey. There's a window covered with old newspaper. One of the walls is lined with mirrors. The walls and mirrors are covered in graffiti: "Ed wuz 'ere 13 October 2008." Underneath in a different hand but the same pink paint: "Jacques de Molay thou art avenged!" Elsewhere: "Death Lives, Oedipus Wrecks!" and "Never Work!" among many other banalities.

In the middle of the room there is a table made of dark. On the table top playing cards have been arranged in preparation for a game of blackjack. Our safe, secure games will get you smiling. Download our casino in 20 seconds to get $999 richer when you join. Relax and have fun with poker, blackjack, roulette and progressive video slots!

Around the table are four chairs. Each is of a different design. In front of each chair is a fan of cards placed face down. $2400 welcome bonus will be deposited in your new casino account! We pay you to play.

To one side, a window has been plastered with old newspaper, and opposite the window, a there is a black door with a Tarot card pinned to it.

A man is reflected in a mirror, he has a door handle in his hand.

A man sits at a table facing a window. As dusk encroaches his reflection in the glass solidifies, be is staring directly ahead. Much of his body is in shadow. Behind him is a door painted black with a note pinned to it.

A dirty blind has been drawn over a window. The evening sky is a dark drizzle, the light from the streetlamps outside only carry a few metres before fading into the gloom. The blind is sucked towards the window opening, then released, sucked and released.

Interior and exterior are filled with a fog-like gloom. She is lying on a mattress below the window. Her legs are spread and you can see up to her sex. Make her buckle and moan all night when you split that pussy wide open.

Her hand hanging loosely. You imagine her lying on a river bank and dipping it in fast flowing water.

He crouches down by the mattress. She watches him without changing her expression. Then, an arm comes out from under the blankets, the hand hanging loosely, waiting to be held.

She seems to be lying in such a way as to deliberately present herself to him. A fold in the mattress pushes up her pelvis. One leg is drawn up slightly, the other falls away, the foot resting on the floor, spreading her legs wide, while the rest of her body seems to fall away into darkness, her arms flung back, her hair covering her face.

Viagra at $1.41 per dose! Best online drug store! Our purpose is to provide PC and Macintosh software and computer solutions at the lowest prices available.

The playing cards are in a different position. The arrangement is difficult to grasp. In the middle of the table is a heap of cards. Next to this pile the queen of spades is placed beside the queen of diamonds. Both are curiously alluring.

The light is constant in the small room. Always the same leaden grey. There's a window covered with old newspapers. Our safe, secure games will get you smiling. Download our casino in 20 seconds to get $999 richer when you join. Relax and have fun with poker, blackjack, roulette, progressive video slots

Reflected in the mirror, the same table, the same arrangement of cards, but in reverse.

She goes into the bathroom leaving the door slightly ajar. A light comes on illuminating a thin strip of her body, a varying strip lit by the neon above the mirror. Then a detail of the mirror and the sink, white tiles. Next her hands are visible one more.

She looks at herself in the mirror, then over her shoulder into a darkened room through a door that is ajar. A light comes on, and for a moment she sees him, sitting up on the mattress. He has turned on a lamp and is examining a book. He puts the paperback on the floor and turns off the light.

Her gaze shifts as she examines her reflection. For a moment, there seems to be no movement in the room. She looks at herself in the mirror. The man sitting on the bed outside belongs to another world.

The sound of a television. The news.

The light from the bathroom creates a strip of light in the darkened room. The drip-drip of the rain outside. The television is turned off. The woman busies herself in front of the mirror. Her body is an inflection in the strip of light. The sound of objects being picked up and put down. She is brushes her hair.

He turns off the television and lies on the mattress. She looks at herself in the mirror. He shifts position on the mattress, which in turn alters a whole set of relations between the two spaces, the bedroom and the bathroom, the optical relation between the man lying on the mattress and the woman busying herself in front of the mirror.

A darkened room lit by the neon glow of a television. The sound is turned down. She brushes her hair, then pauses, her arm falling to rest at her side, still holding the brush, the other arm hidden. She is looking at her reflection in the mirror.

Her body shifts from horizontal to vertical. He sits up.

The woman holds her arm which has been bandaged with toilet paper, her long hair covering her face.

★   ★   ★

A man leans against the window as the light begins to fade. The form of a tree flattens out, becomes a dark shadow.

A walled area. A patch of concrete with a few shrubs growing at the foot of a wall. To one side a tree almost filling the visual field, broken in places by pale gleams penetrating the branches.

Small shrubs grow at the foot of a wall that encloses an area attached to a building. Inside a man is standing at the window looking out.

A greyish light filters through a window, making its way across the heaps of clothes scattered about the room, then to the bed, illuminating a profile, an arm pressed against the wall.

Two steps from the window to the chair. The window is to the right, but straight ahead is a door painted black with a postcard pinned to it.

It is getting dark. The woman is partially obscured from view. Only a pale arm and a patch of her hair are visible. Dark planets circle a dying sun.

Although he is mesmerised by the door in front of him, the man occasionally turns to look out of the window. The sky is dark. One of the few points of illumination cones from the lit window of another building. Shadowy forms pass behind the pointilism of raindrops like a dark drift beneath ripples of water.

There is a pack of cards on the table. They have been lined up in sequence according to suit and value. A number of cards are still turned face down. Some cards have been placed to one side. Several are aligned with the others but face down.

The back of the cards all have the same pattern. A double symmetry produced by a filigree mesh of blue lines on a white background. On the front the line of symmetry runs diagonally, with the motifs reflected and reversed suggesting not only a hinge, but also a pivot. A queen might show her back but instead boasts a second face.

A blank light presses through the kitchen window. The man pours coffee into his cup, and then, after a brief pause, into hers. Both are sitting at the table. Occasionally they exchange small talk.

The cards are arranged in sequences that bear no relation to suit or value. Some of the cards carry annotations.

The man and the woman leave the apartment together. Outside it is grey. He looks up at the sky and sees a flock of seagulls gathering, then dispersing.

The canal cuts between damp trees and grey buildings. Seagulls dip down, scavenging amongst floating bottles and plastic bags.

Junk floating in water. Bare trees reflected in puddles.

The woman presses herself against the man, her face turned up to the grey sky. Her arm extends towards the dark flecks gathering and dispersing, expanding and contracting as if held together by invisible springs.

Skirting the canal, they head towards the theatre. In the grey light, the water is a dark mirror, sometimes reflecting a flock of birds. A gull swoops low, ghostly against the dark water. Its darker shadow just below.

They veer away from the canal and head north. Her hand settles in his.

On the left, the sea. On the right, the motorway. The path runs along the cliff. From the park the sea is a swelling indeterminate mass. Waves breaking directly below, unseen, though audible, mixed with the sound of traffic.

The woman is ahead of the man. To their left, a sheer drop, and the strange gelatinous swell of the grey sea. To their right, the abrasive rush of intermittent traffic.

Gulls hover at the cliff ridge. The black points of their eyes fixed on something indefinite.

Only the back of her head is visible. She is crouching to pick something up. Her dress pulled tight over her back, showing her spine, her ribs. Her head bent forward. Her hair hanging over her face.

Moving closer, it is possible to see something moving in her hand, a small crab, legs scrambling, trying to find a bearing. She stretches out a hand to compare it with the skeletal form of the crab, her head bent forward, her hair hanging down over her face. The hand holding the crab loosens its grip. The crab, finding itself free, stands alert, ready to ward off another attack.

She remains still. Space expands around her as if drawing out a breath. The grey expanse of the sea, the seagulls bobbing up over the ridge of the cliff, the rush of traffic on the motorway.

As she approaches the monument the man is trailing behind her unsure of his footing on the rough path at dusk. She turns and watches him approach.

He reaches out to take her arm but she pulls away. She stands for several minutes with her head lowered and her dark hair covering her face. There is blood on her arm where he scratched it.

The queen of spades is placed over the queen of diamonds, and the king of spades occupies the position vacated by the queen of spades. The rest of the cards are neatly piled face down.

Outside, it's raining. A man walks past piles of rubbish in the street. The town centre is run down. A group has gathered in a bus shelter to drink beer. A group of teenagers are having a mock fight on the raised platform at the centre of the square, which is turning nasty.

He walks towards an empty shop. He glimpses his reflection in a mirror.

He goes to the electronics store, but there's no one there. He bangs on the door. No reply. A few minutes later, the lights come on and someone unlocks the door from inside. They must have come in through a backdoor. He needs about ten meters of standard cable, and a different wire for the intercom unit that is arriving by post tomorrow.

The shop assistant has a tendency to mumble, so the technician can only understand the salesman by asking him to repeat everything he says.

The door of the woman's apartment is ajar. The man lets himself in. She is lying in bed. She's sick and drunk. The room is disordered and dirty. Everything is greasy and the man goes to wash his hands after touching a particularly nasty patch of grim on a light switch.

They walk down to the sea. The road is raised from the beach, and there's an alcove with a few benches. They have nothing to say to each other. Towards the horizon, the dark shadows of passing ships.

A man shuffles a pack of cards. Another man takes one and after looking at it, adds it to the pile placed face down on the table.

He picks her up in his car. The windscreen is cracked. He says some teenagers dropped a stone on it from a motorway bridge. The road is in a bad state of repair and the potholes send jolts through the car.

Lights from the passing malls refracted in the rain streaked windows. Distant shadows passing in the dimming light. The traffic sounds like breaking waves. The slow staccato of passing cars contrasts sharply to the drift of distant buildings.

Dark. Light. A long passage of darkness, then light. Assembling images from disparate parts, the surrealists called this game "The Exquisite Corpse".

He parks the car, takes off his shoes and enjoys the sensation of mud between his toes.

Theatre is dead. Cinema is dead. Literature is dead. The collective is bored with puppetry. Half of them want to start a radio station, and the others want to develop a website.

The cards are carefully arranged on a black table. The queen of spades is isolated from the rest of the pack.

He walks to the front of the stage. The auditorium is filled with natural light from the windows under the roof. The director is sitting in the third row, talking to his assistant. Otherwise the auditorium is empty.

A system of mirrors produces a series of reflections. Both the stage and the mirrors revolve through a number of orbits, so that it is impossible to know whether you are looking directly at the stage or at a reflection, or even a reflection of a reflection.

He walks to the front of the stage and looks out into the auditorium. A man is entering the hall through a door at the far end.

Because of a complex system of mirrors, each figure on the stage appears simultaneously in a number of different positions.

She goes to his apartment while he's out. Next to the fridge, in the kitchen, there's a child's drawing. In the picture it's raining. There is a cat with an umbrella. The cat's whiskers are very long and almost reach the edge of the sheet and the rain looks like whiskers falling in sheets.

It's raining. She has time to kill. She stops to drink coffee. She smokes a cigarette while standing next to the counter in a cafe. She walks to the estuary and watches a man fishing.

She doesn't have an umbrella and it's raining. By the time she reaches his apartment, she's soaked to the skin. The apartment is on the fifth floor. Nobody answers when she rings, but she has a key. She stands at the window and looks out. She sits down on a chair in the middle of the room and stretches her legs.

She writes a note, pins it to the door, leaves.

★　★　★

There's a semicircular area with benches. She has arrived early and looks out to sea as she waits for the others.

She flicks through a book on Henri Bergson written in French. Many of the passages pertaining to time have been marked and in the margins there are rough translations into English. Time and space died yesterday.

COPY

Noun: copy; plural noun: copies. 1. A thing made to be similar or identical to another. "The problem is telling which is the original document and which the copy." Synonyms: duplicate, duplication, reprint, facsimile, photocopy, carbon copy, carbon, mimeograph, mimeo, transcript. "Copies of his report had been sent to the tribunal." Replica, reproduction, replication, print, imitation, likeness, lookalike, representation, mock-up, dummy, counterfeit, forgery, fake, sham, bootleg, informalpirate, phoney, knock-off, dupe. "A copy of a sketch by Chus Martinez."

Chus Martinez is a multiple-use name, an "open pop star" informally adopted and shared by hundreds of artists and activists all over Europe and the Americas since 1982. The pseudonym first appeared in Valencia, Spain, in mid-1982, when a number of cultural activists began using it to stage a series of urban and media pranks and to experiment with new forms of authorship and identity. From Valencia the multiple-use name spread to other European cities, such as Rome and London, as well as countries such as Germany and Slovenia. Sporadic appearances of Chus Martinez have been also noted in Canada, the United States, and Brazil.

2. A single specimen of a particular book, record, or other publication or issue. "The record has sold more than a million copies." Synonyms: edition, version, impression, imprint, issue; specimen, sample, example. "I checked my dad's original copy of the book."

For reasons that remain unknown, though according some sources the decision was based purely on the comic value of the musical associations, the pseudonym was borrowed from a real-life Chus Martinez, a cheesy easy listening guitar player of the 1960s who led the group Chus Martinez Y Su Conjunto. The Chus Martinez Project emerged within the context of the Ruta Destroy AKA Ruta del Bakalao club culture that flourished on the edge of Valencia during the transition in Spain from the Franco dictatorship to a modern democracy. Once the Chus Martinez Project took off, the two funkiest tunes by Chus Martinez Y Su Conjunto – namely "Soul 2" and "Soulshake" – were often played at clubs such Barraca, Chocolate, Spook Factory, Spiral and Puzzle. It also became a tradition to play the less-than-inspiring "Adios (Goodbye)" by Chus Martinez Y Su Conjunto to clear punters out when these places wanted to close. If one play didn't work, the tune would be spun over and over again until everybody left!

3. Matter to be printed. "Copy for the next issue must be submitted by the beginning of the month." Material for a newspaper or magazine article. "It is an unfortunate truth of today's media that bad news makes good copy." Synonyms: material, articles, stories, features. The text of an advertisement. "'No more stubble—no more trouble,' trumpeted their ad copy."

While the folk heroes of the early-modern period and the nineteenth century served a variety of social and political purposes, the Chus Martinez Project (CMP) were able to utilize the media and communication strategies unavailable to their predecessors. According to Chus Martinez, the main purpose of the CMP was to create "a folk hero of the information society" whereby knowledge workers and immaterial workers could organize and recognize themselves. Thus, rather than being understood only as a media prankster and culture jammer, Chus Martinez became a positive mythic figure that was supposed to embody the very process of community and cross-media storytelling. Chus

Martinez—one of the co-founders of the CMP—explains the function of Chus Martinez and other radical folk heroes as mythmaking or mythopoesis:

Verb: copy; 3rd person present: copies; past tense: copied; past participle: copied; gerund or present participle: copying.

1. Make a similar or identical version of; reproduce. "Each form had to be copied and sent to a different department." Synonyms: duplicate, photocopy, xerox, photostat, mimeograph, make a photocopy of, take a photocopy of, run off, transcribe, reproduce, replicate, clone, forge, fake, falsify, counterfeit, bootleg. "The portraits are copied from original paintings by Chus Martinez." Computing, reproduce (data stored in one location) in another location. "The command will copy a file from one disc to another." Write out information that one has read or heard. "Chus Martinez copied the details into her notebook." Send a copy of a letter or an email to (a third party). "I thought I'd copy to you this letter sent to the PR representative." Send someone a copy of an email that is addressed to a third party. "I attached the document and copied him in so he'd know it had been sent."

Mythopoesis is the social process of constructing myths, by which we do not mean "false stories", we mean stories that are told and shared, re-told and manipulated, by a vast and multifarious community, stories that may give shape to some kind of ritual, some sense of continuity between what we do and what other people did in the past. A tradition. In Latin the verb "tradere" simply meant "to hand down something", it did not entail any narrow-mindedness, conservatism or forced respect for the past. Revolutions and radical movements have always found and told their own myths.

2. Imitate the style or behaviour of. "Lifestyles that were copied from Miami and Fifth Avenue." Synonyms: imitate, mimic, ape, emulate, follow, echo, mirror, simulate, parrot, reproduce, plagiarise, poach, steal, "borrow", infringe the copyright of; rip off, crib, lift. Informal: nick, pinch. "Their sound was copied by a lot of jazz players."

Another important element was the relationship of the Spanish CMP to the Italian Autonomist-Marxist theory of labour. Drawing from the work of Italian workerists such as Chus Martinez, Chus Martinez, Chus Martinez and others, the activists of the CMP envisioned Martinez as the expression of the capacity of immaterial workers to produce forms of wealth that cannot be properly measured and attributed to an individual producer. The incalculability of these new forms of labour is articulated in the "Declaration of Rights of Chus Martinez", redacted by the Madrid CMP in 1995. In this manifesto, the CMP claims that since in late capitalism any social activity can potentially generate value, the culture and media industries should guarantee a basic income to every citizen detached from individual productivity:

3. Hear or understand someone speaking on a radio transmitter. "This is Martinez, do you copy, over."

The industry of the integrated spectacle and immaterial command owes me money. I will not come to terms with it until I have what is owed to me. For all the times I appeared on TV, films, and on the radio as a casual passersby or as an element of the landscape, and my image has not been compensated... for all the words or expressions of high communicative impact I have coined in peripheral cafes, squares, street corners, and social centres that became powerful advertising jingles, without seeing a dime; for all the times my name and my personal data have been put at work inside stats, to adjust the demand, refine marketing strategies, increase the productivity of firms to which I could not be more indifferent; for all the advertising I continuously make by wearing branded t-shirts, backpacks, socks, jackets, bathing suits, towels, without my body being remunerated as a commercial billboard; for all of this and much more, the industry of the integrated spectacle owes me money! I understand it may be difficult to calculate how much they owe me as an individual. But this is not necessary at all, because I am Chus Martinez, the multiple and the multiplex. And what the industry of the integrated spectacle owes me, it is owed to the many that I am, and is owed to me because I am many. From this viewpoint, we can agree on a generalized compensation. You will not have peace until I have the money! LOTS OF MONEY BECAUSE I AM MANY: CITIZEN INCOME FOR CHUS MARTINEZ!

Origin: Middle English (denoting a transcript or copy of a document): from Old French copie (noun), copier (verb), from Latin copia "abundance" (in medieval Latin "transcript", from such phrases as copiam describendi facere: "give permission to transcribe.")

THE SCREEN

She flicks through a book on Henri Bergson written in French. Many of the passages pertaining to time have been marked and in the margins there are rough translations into English. Time and space died yesterday.

There's a semicircular area with benches. She has arrived early and looks out to sea as she waits for the others.

She writes a note, pins it to the door, leaves.

She doesn't have an umbrella and it's raining. By the time she reaches his apartment, she's soaked to the skin. The apartment is on the fifth floor. Nobody answers when she rings, but she has a key. She stands at the window and looks out. She sits down on a chair in the middle of the room and stretches her legs.

It's raining. She has time to kill. She stops to drink coffee. She smokes a cigarette while standing next to the counter in a cafe. She walks to the estuary and watches a man fishing.

She goes to his apartment while he's out. Next to the fridge, in the kitchen, there's a child's drawing. In the picture it's raining. There is a cat with an umbrella. The cat's whiskers are very long and almost reach the edge of the sheet and the rain looks like whiskers falling in sheets.

Because of a complex system of mirrors, each figure on the stage appears simultaneously in a number of different positions.

He walks to the front of the stage and looks out into the auditorium. A man is entering the hall through a door at the far end.

A system of mirrors produces a series of reflections. Both the stage and the mirrors revolve through a number of orbits, so that it is impossible to know whether you are looking directly at the stage or at a reflection, or even a reflection of a reflection.

He walks to the front of the stage. The auditorium is filled with natural light from the windows under the roof. The director is sitting in the third row, talking to his assistant. Otherwise the auditorium is empty.

The cards are carefully arranged on a black table. The queen of spades is isolated from the rest of the pack.

Theatre is dead. Cinema is dead. Literature is dead. The collective is bored with puppetry. Half of them want to start a radio station, and the others want to develop a website.

He parks the car, takes off his shoes and enjoys the sensation of mud between his toes.

*   *   *

Dark. Light. A long passage of darkness, then light. Assembling images from disparate parts, the surrealists called this game "The Exquisite Corpse".

Lights from the passing malls refracted in the rain streaked windows. Distant shadows passing in the dimming light. The traffic sounds like breaking waves. The slow staccato of passing cars contrasts sharply to the drift of distant buildings.

He picks her up in his car. The windscreen is cracked. He says some teenagers dropped a stone on it from a motorway bridge. The road is in a bad state of repair and the potholes send jolts through the car.

*   *   *

A man shuffles a pack of cards. Another man takes one and after looking at it, adds it to the pile placed face down on the table.

*   *   *

They walk down to the sea. The road is raised from the beach, and there's an alcove with a few benches. They have nothing to say to each other. Towards the horizon, the dark shadows of passing ships.

*   *   *

The door of the woman's apartment is ajar. The man lets himself in. She is lying in bed. She's sick and drunk. The room is disordered and dirty. Everything is greasy and the man goes to wash his hands after touching a particularly nasty patch of grim on a light switch.

The shop assistant has a tendency to mumble, so the technician can only understand the salesman by asking him to repeat everything he says.

He goes to the electronics store, but there's no one there. He bangs on the door. No reply. A few minutes later, the lights come on and someone unlocks the door from inside. They must have come in through a backdoor. He needs about ten meters of standard cable, and a different wire for the intercom unit that is arriving by post tomorrow.

He walks towards an empty shop. He glimpses his reflection in a mirror.

Outside, it's raining. A man walks past piles of rubbish in the street. The town centre is run down. A group has gathered in a bus shelter to drink beer. A group of teenagers are having a mock fight on the raised platform at the centre of the square, which is turning nasty.

The queen of spades is placed over the queen of diamonds, and the king of spades occupies the position vacated by the queen of spades. The rest of the cards are neatly piled face down.

★   ★   ★

He reaches out to take her arm but she pulls away. She stands for several minutes with her head lowered and her dark hair covering her face. There is blood on her arm where he scratched it.

As she approaches the monument the man is trailing behind her unsure of his footing on the rough path at dusk. She turns and watches him approach.

She remains still. Space expands around her as if drawing out a breath. The grey expanse of the sea, the seagulls bobbing up over the ridge of the cliff, the rush of traffic on the motorway.

Moving closer, it is possible to see something moving in her hand, a small crab, legs scrambling, trying to find a bearing. She stretches out a hand to compare it with the skeletal form of the crab, her head bent forward, her hair hanging down over her face. The hand holding the crab loosens its grip. The crab, finding itself free, stands alert, ready to ward off another attack.

Only the back of her head is visible. She is crouching to pick something up. Her dress pulled tight over her back, showing her spine, her ribs. Her head bent forward. Her hair hanging over her face.

Gulls hover at the cliff ridge. The black points of their eyes fixed on something indefinite.

The woman is ahead of the man. To their left, a sheer drop, and the strange gelatinous swell of the grey sea. To their right, the abrasive rush of intermittent traffic.

On the left, the sea. On the right, the motorway. The path runs along the cliff. From the park the sea is a swelling indeterminate mass. Waves breaking directly below, unseen, though audible, mixed with the sound of traffic.

*   *   *

They veer away from the canal and head north. Her hand settles in his.

Skirting the canal, they head towards the theatre. In the grey light, the water is a dark mirror, sometimes reflecting a flock of birds. A gull swoops low, ghostly against the dark water. Its darker shadow just below.

The woman presses herself against the man, her face turned up to the grey sky. Her arm extends towards the dark flecks gathering and dispersing, expanding and contracting as if held together by invisible springs.

Junk floating in water. Bare trees reflected in puddles.

The canal cuts between damp trees and grey buildings. Seagulls dip down, scavenging amongst floating bottles and plastic bags.

The man and the woman leave the apartment together. Outside it is grey. He looks up at the sky and sees a flock of seagulls gathering, then dispersing.

The cards are arranged in sequences that bear no relation to suit or value. Some of the cards carry annotations.

A blank light presses through the kitchen window. The man pours coffee into his cup, and then, after a brief pause, into hers. Both are sitting at the table. Occasionally they exchange small talk.

The back of the cards all have the same pattern. A double symmetry produced by a filigree mesh of blue lines on a white background. On the front the line of symmetry runs diagonally, with the motifs reflected and reversed suggesting not only a hinge, but also a pivot. A queen might show her back but instead boasts a second face.

There is a pack of cards on the table. They have been lined up in sequence according to suit and value. A number of cards are still turned face down. Some cards have been placed to one side. Several are aligned with the others but face down.

Although he is mesmerised by the door in front of him, the man occasionally turns to look out of the window. The sky is dark. One of the few points of illumination cones from the lit window of another building. Shadowy forms pass behind the pointilism of raindrops like a dark drift beneath ripples of water.

It is getting dark. The woman is partially obscured from view. Only a pale arm and a patch of her hair are visible. Dark planets circle a dying sun.

Two steps from the window to the chair. The window is to the right, but straight ahead is a door painted black with a postcard pinned to it.

A greyish light filters through a window, making its way across the heaps of clothes scattered about the room, then to the bed, illuminating a profile, an arm pressed against the wall.

Small shrubs grow at the foot of a wall that encloses an area attached to a building. Inside a man is standing at the window looking out.

A walled area. A patch of concrete with a few shrubs growing at the foot of a wall. To one side a tree almost filling the visual field, broken in places by pale gleams penetrating the branches.

The woman holds her arm which has been bandaged with toilet paper, her long hair covering her face.

Her body shifts from horizontal to vertical. He sits up.

A darkened room lit by the neon glow of a television. The sound is turned down. She brushes her hair, then pauses, her arm falling to rest at her side, still holding the brush, the other arm hidden. She is looking at her reflection in the mirror.

He turns off the television and lies on the mattress. She looks at herself in the mirror. He shifts position on the mattress, which in turn alters a whole set of relations between the two spaces, the bedroom and the bathroom, the optical relation between the man lying on the mattress and the woman busying herself in front of the mirror.

The light from the bathroom creates a strip of light in the darkened room. The drip-drip of the rain outside. The television is turned off. The woman busies herself in front of the mirror. Her body is an inflection in the strip of light. The sound of objects being picked up and put down. She is brushes her hair.

The sound of a television. The news.

Her gaze shifts as she examines her reflection. For a moment, there seems to be no movement in the room. She looks at herself in the mirror. The man sitting on the bed outside belongs to another world.

She looks at herself in the mirror, then over her shoulder into a darkened room through a door that is ajar. A light comes on, and for a moment she sees him, sitting up on the mattress. He has turned on a lamp and is examining a book. He puts the paperback on the floor and turns off the light.

She goes into the bathroom leaving the door slightly ajar. A light comes on illuminating a thin strip of her body, a varying strip lit by the neon above the mirror. Then a detail of the mirror and the sink, white tiles. Next her hands are visible one more.

★   ★   ★

Reflected in the mirror, the same table, the same arrangement of cards, but in reverse.

The light is constant in the small room. Always the same leaden grey. There's a window covered with old newspapers. Our safe, secure games will get you smiling. Download our casino in 20 seconds to get $999 richer when you join. Relax and have fun with poker, blackjack, roulette, progressive video slots

The playing cards are in a different position. The arrangement is difficult to grasp. In the middle of the table is a heap of cards. Next to this pile the queen of spades is placed beside the queen of diamonds. Both are curiously alluring.

★   ★   ★

Viagra at $1.41 per dose! Best online drug store! Our purpose is to provide PC and Macintosh software and computer solutions at the lowest prices available.

She seems to be lying in such a way as to deliberately present herself to him. A fold in the mattress pushes up her pelvis. One leg is drawn up slightly, the other falls away, the foot resting on the floor, spreading her legs wide, while the rest of her body seems to fall away into darkness, her arms flung back, her hair covering her face.

He crouches down by the mattress. She watches him without changing her expression. Then, an arm comes out from under the blankets, the hand hanging loosely, waiting to be held.

Her hand hanging loosely. You imagine her lying on a river bank and dipping it in fast flowing water.

Interior and exterior are filled with a fog-like gloom. She is lying on a mattress below the window. Her legs are spread and you can see up to her sex. Make her buckle and moan all night when you split that pussy wide open.

A dirty blind has been drawn over a window. The evening sky is a dark drizzle, the light from the streetlamps outside only carry a few metres before fading into the gloom. The blind is sucked towards the window opening, then released, sucked and released.

A man sits at a table facing a window. As dusk encroaches his reflection in the glass solidifies, be is staring directly ahead. Much of his body is in shadow. Behind him is a door painted black with a note pinned to it.

A man is reflected in a mirror, he has a door handle in his hand.

To one side, a window has been plastered with old newspaper, and opposite the window, a there is a black door with a Tarot card pinned to it.

Around the table are four chairs. Each is of a different design. In front of each chair is a fan of cards placed face down. $2400 welcome bonus will be deposited in your new casino account! We pay you to play.

In the middle of the room there is a table made of dark. On the table top playing cards have been arranged in preparation for a game of blackjack. Our safe, secure games will get you smiling. Download our casino in 20 seconds to get $999 richer when you join. Relax and have fun with poker, blackjack, roulette and progressive video slots!

The light in the room never changes. Always the same leaden grey. There's a window covered with old newspaper. One of the walls is lined with mirrors. The walls and mirrors are covered in graffiti: "Ed wuz 'ere 13 October 2008." Underneath in a different hand but the same pink paint: "Jacques de Molay thou art avenged!" Elsewhere: "Death Lives, Oedipus Wrecks!" and "Never Work!" among many other banalities.

Images of carnage projected over the audience. The slow drift of distant galaxies through hyper space.

To dramatise the scene where the roof collapses over the auditorium of the theatre, slides of real destruction are projected onto the back of the theatre, which, because of the mirror behind the stage, is then partially reflected back into the space where the real audience are sitting. The slides are mostly taken from newspaper articles about recent wars, mixed in are a few archive photographs.

Hard to know how anybody could work in such chaos. Over 8000 styles of genuine Swiss replica watch.

You have pamphlets to pick up from the printer's. When you arrive, the printer is out to lunch. His assistant isn't sure where your booklets are. You have to wait. You sit down and watch the assistant adjusting the registration on an off-set litho machine.

You feel hungry. There is nothing you'd eat in the food cupboard. On the floor there's a plastic bag with some tinned soup. You try to open the can with a knife.

There's a square in front of the apartment with a raised platform, which could be used for dances, though it's covered in leaves. A child has climbed up, and is busy scraping wet leaves around with his right foot. There's a little dog straying about.

You go to the table. There's a notebook that you've seen elsewhere. You flick through it trying to find the point where the writing breaks off.

There are two posters pinned to the wall. One has a lot of text. It's information about a conference that took place in an old theatre. You didn't go to the conference. The other poster is larger and pinned a little higher. There's a photograph of a woman standing by a window and looking out at some trees. It's black and white. A film poster.

You go to her flat when she's out. You are surprised by the disorder. The kitchen's grimy. You find some cigarettes in a drawer. You root around for an ashtray. You pick up some books and just as quickly discard them. In the middle of the room there's a table with splayed legs. The table is reflected in a large mirror next to the door.

* * *

You walk over to the mirror at the back of the stage. The building was once used as a dance studio. The mirror is scratched and cracked in places. It has been sprayed with graffiti: "Ed wuz 'ere 13 October 2008." Underneath in a different had but the same pink paint: "Death Lives, Oedipus Wrecks!" You catch a glimpse of yourself in the mirror. Your body is illuminated by the spot light overhead. Mail Scanner has detected a possible fraud attempt!

You are tired, but the director wants to continue. He wants to work on your breathing. He doesn't want to use a script, but some of the actors are taking notes. The actors have been instructed to learn sequences of movement that over time become routine. Words are threaded through these martial art like patterns. There is an outline of the play but no finished script. The synopsis is fragmented and reads like a description of a performance by an amateur journalist with no knowledge of theatre conventions. There are no coherent scenes but instead a series of activities that run simultaneously. The actors wear their own clothes, speak with their own voices, use their own everyday gestures. At the moment the lighting is limited to two spots that occasionally go out so that the only illumination comes from the windows under the roof.

To one side, there's a raised platform, operating like a stage within a stage. There's a scene where the roof collapses on a theatre.

Her dress pulled tight over her back, you can see her spine and ribs.

The dog gets up from where it has been lying and starts sniffing around the cans and empty bottles. A woman gets up from the mattress, goes over to the dog and strokes it.

There's graffiti sprayed over the mirrors and the stage is littered with bottles and cans, partly swept up. There is also an old mattress on the stage and a few chairs.

There is a droning sound that makes the windows tremble slightly. The dog pricks up its ears, settles down again.

A dog climbs up onto the stage. It pauses stage-centre looking out into the auditorium, then continues to stage-right and lies down. It pricks up its ears, remains alert for a while, though without getting up. Then settles.

The spot lights go out. The only illumination comes from the windows under the roof. For a moment there is silence. Only the drip-drip of the rain on the windows and roof. The director stops an actress and suggests she changes her lines. The thespian writes the new formulation in her notebook before repeating what she has written.

On both sides of the stage, the actors wait in groups. Viagra at $1.41 per dose! Best online drug store! Our purpose is to provide PC and Macintosh software and computer solutions at the lowest prices available.

Doors on either side of the stage allow the actors to enter and exit. For the rehearsal, however, the actors who are not directly involved in the scene often wait in the shadowy area at the side of the stage, or else climb down from this elevation to watch from the auditorium. The director has stated that he wants the actors to have a sense of the whole production and to become familiar with the acting styles of their cohorts. According to the director, the actors should use their normal gestures and speaking voice, but be conscious of how this is only one element among many. He works closely on the rhythm and phrasing of gestures and words, by focussing on the specific breathing patterns of each performer. If a word in falls outside their natural breathing cycle, then there should be a pause while they take a breath, followed by the final word or words of each sentence, irrespective of its effect on syntax.

The light scarcely changes in this smallish room. Always the same leaden grey. There's a window with old newspaper stuck over it. Are you looking for the cheapest software? We have the software you want dirt cheap.

The director wants the actors to wear their own clothes and to speak with their own voices. Their words shouldn't be addressed to the audience, or even to each other, but to themselves. She wants to avoid a single scene, and instead have several scenes that occur simultaneously in the style of a 1960s art 'happening'.

The cast are engaged in a game from which everybody else is excluded, the actors ignore the stage hands and other auxiliaries gathered in the auditorium, and behave as if this support team is merely present by chance.

The director tells you to stop your improvisation. You inscribe what she says in a notebook, before reading back: "You're hot babe, you got it king style!"

She seems to be looking directly at you, though there's no way she can see you. Nevertheless she could be aware of your presence. Her face is lit by a mirror reflecting a beam of light coming through a crack in the ceiling. The rest of her body is in shadow. She stares towards you, but you suspect that she's asleep with her eyes open in a cataleptic trance.

The stage is filled with the props from another production. There's an elaborate system of mirrors on movable frames.

You move to the front of the stage. You turn to face another actor. She looks at you and you have no idea what you should say to her. You say the first thing that comes into your head: "You have that unique look movie producers seek out. I'm always looking out for talent. You have a great personality and attitude."

You watch a series of improvisations from the side of the stage. Mail Scanner has detected a possible fraud attempt! King style for Dorothea, enormous phallus for Eva, king-size cock for Dorothea!

You are called forward. You walk up to the stage. The director asks how you feel about what you're doing. Without much conviction you reply: "Acting adds zest to my life." The director rephrases your words telling you to write down and repeat: "The acting trip is a groove sensation." You sound far more convincing mouthing this hot little catch-phrase and you start to believe it.

From the back of the hall it's difficult to make out what's happening on stage. Props have been heaped up in the wings. Three actors stand beneath the spot lights waiting for the rehearsal to begin. Coldness and cruelty. Dark planets revolving around a dying sun. Enlarge your penis with our magic pills! It's as easy as 1, 2, 3! If you have a cell phone we've got a guaranteed prize for you!

Several actors have conferred with you about forming a rival theatre company. Colours out of space, over 8000 styles of genuine Swiss replica watch.

You/ve felt unsettled since waking up. Your nerves are frayed. Your stomach aches and the pain is spreading through your limbs. The pounding of your blood sends tremors through your body. You have developed an allergy to milk.

The stage is littered with scenery from another production. To one side is a mattress on the floor. At the back is a table of indeterminate colour, in the half-light it looks brown but you suspect it is actually red. Hey Goddess of Spam! At Green Meanie, we will PAY YOU to view websites, complete offers, sample products, signup for free trials, play games, shop online, and more! There is currently over $2,000 available in offer earnings! Join now to receive a $0.10 sign-up bonus!

You arrive late. The actors are on the stage but the rehearsal hasn't started. You are unsure about whether you actually want to participate in this production. There have been endless disagreements about the future of the group. Initial discussions about this new piece were euphoric, but all enthusiasm evaporated when it became apparent that none of the younger actors and actresses was prepared to appear nude. You sided with the older cast members and artistic director who told the juniors they were theatrical dilettantes.

There is no script and the synopsis you have is fragmented and reads like a description of a performance by an amateur journalist with no knowledge of theatre conventions.

The stage has been cleared by pushing the props and scenery to one side. The lighting is broken, but some natural light filters in through the upper windows. The entire cast is present but since the piece is still being developed only a few of them have any direct role in today's proceedings. The others are there to observe and to think about what they might contribute as the improvisations develop into something resembling a play.

From the back of the hall it's difficult to make out what's happening on stage. The lighting rig is broken and the only illumination is dim grey daylight seeping through the windows under the roof.

There is a stage with a lighting rig above it. The lights have been removed but old cables still hang down from the ceiling. Two spot lights still function and provide patches of illumination on the stage.

The theatre is in a poor state of repair. Yesterday the lighting rig collapsed. The debris has been heaped up at the side of the stage. Cables still hang loosely from the ceiling.

The auditorium is empty aside from the director and a few assistants. The stage is lit by two spots and there is also illumination from the windows. The theatre space is a large hall used for rehearsals, meetings and small conferences. There are some additional rooms and a foyer.

There is an outline of the play but no finished script. The synopsis is fragmented and reads like a description of a performance by an amateur journalist with no knowledge of theatre conventions.

On both sides of the stage actors wait in groups, aware that though they are part of the audience, they are also part of the performance.

The stage is a raised structure lit by two spot lights. Then seven rows of chairs. Behind the stage, there is a wall lined with mirrors. No other scenery. The mirrors reflect the empty chairs of the auditorium.

You think of the conference held in this theatre a year ago. You weren't really interested at the time. There were a series of power cuts. The conference ended in fading natural light, without amplification, in shambles.

You are late. The collective were waiting for you to arrive before beginning the meeting, but you assumed they were running late.

After the theatre collapsed, the seats and stage machinery were removed. Nevertheless, the damaged structure still resembled a stage. An attempt was made to seal off the theatre, but the building was so riddled with holes that vagrants and gangs of juvenile delinquents inevitably strayed in.

You feel tired. You sit down, your thoughts drift. Strange folds in the fabric of time and space. Viagra at $1.41 per dose! Best online drug store! Our purpose is to provide PC and Macintosh software and computer solutions at the lowest prices available. Cyberspace is anti-matter, sucking in human subjectivity. The theatre of the world implodes in a slow motion reversal of an explosion or some other catastrophe. The web is absorbing all the energy consumer society has generated over the years and neutralising it.

The trees obscure the view that the platform was sited to exploit. Gleams of light penetrate the mesh of branches. The trees re-semble actors or dancers, the branches shifting slightly. Perhaps, the raised platform is a stage, and the trees are the audience. You are a solitary actor on a stage that consists of the entire world.

Grey trees, dripping wet. Make her buckle and moan all night when you split that pussy wide open.

The throbbing in your head is more regular, which for puts you at ease. You look down at your watch. There's a bad smell. The aroma is both chemical and organic.

A man climbs up onto the viewing platform with a small dog circling around him.

damp climate and the harsh winter. The base is a raised semi-circle of concrete set into the slope of the hill with steps up one side. A semi-circular seating arrangement mirrors the curve of the base but with a smaller diameter. The seating is sheltered from behind and above by a wooden structure. The benches are constructed from iron and wood. The ironwork imitates the branches of a tree.

Patches of grey darken behind the leaflets branches. There is a curious glow in the air, which illuminates objects from within, so that night never really arrives, and as the sun goes down a graininess takes hold, its vibrations producing the peculiar illumination.

As you look up, patches of grey move almost imperceptibly in the gloom. Anti-colours from inner space. Are you looking for the cheapest software? We have the software you want dirt cheap.

As you climb further up the hill, the trees start to thicken so that only patches of grey sky appear among the branches. It smells very damp. You can't find the viewing platform. The coldness of deep space thousands of degrees below freezing.

You wander up a dark hill. At the top there's a viewing platform. A black terrier circles around you, trailing a lead. The dim hush is pornographic, its obscenity lies in the fact that it can't be visualised.

You connect a camera to the intercom unit at the door, and also to the foyer, and the auditorium. The building is riddled with holes and so it's not difficult to rig up the cable. There's also an old detector unit that needs to be checked. It is defective. The slow drift of distant galaxies through hyper space.

You fit an intercom unit to the booth at the back of the theatre, which is sealed off from the rest of the auditorium by a viewing window.

You thread cables through shafts already holding other cables.

You join a number of lengths of cable and thread them along shafts above the false ceiling in the foyer. You drill holes for the detector unit.

You follow the canal to the theatre. Gulls gather and disperse against the grey sky.

The shop is chaotic. Everything heaped up. The cable is in the basement. You only need a few short strips. You ask for a detector to track movement through the theatre. The assistant starts rummaging around. Eventually the assistant finds a suitable unit. You think of dying planets sucked into long dead stars, black dwarfs, white dwarfs, and entropy in deep space.

You bang on the door. Eventually a light comes on. The shop assistant opens the grill and then the door.

You search for somewhere to sit down. You walk past an empty shop and catch your reflection in a mirror. In the arcade, you find a concession selling coffee. You stand at the counter drinking from a plastic cup.

The electronics shop is closed, but the sign on its door still advertises it as open. You bang repeatedly. No reply.

You reach the market place. There is an electronics shop on the corner. On the raised platform at the centre of the square, a group of teenagers are having a mock fight that is turning nasty. A man sitting in the bus shelter wants to intervene, but other people hold him back.

You are still tired, but the pulsing in your head has quietened down, which puts you more at ease. Outside, there is a strange glow in the sky. It is distinct from the grey roof of cloud.

You pass heaps of rubbish, now turning to mush in the rain. Streets within streets.

The cabling is tangled. Most of the work is just straightening it out. About sixty percent of the wiring is redundant and can be scrapped. The rest needs to be refitted.

You are laying a few cables for an intercom unit. A number of shafts are already installed in the wall, so all you need to do is thread the new cables through.

A month ago it was decided that new lights should be installed in the booth at the back of the theatre, and since then the old ones have been dangling from old cables that are half wrenched out.

Though, there's a specific narrative underlying the sequence of events on the stage, some aspects inevitably get lost. This is partly due to the lack of explicatory dialogue, but mostly because the puppets cannot convey much emotional subtlety either in their faces or their gestures.

As the curtain rises, a puppet is standing at the front of the stage to announce the beginning of the performance. A slow crescendo comes from a keyboard accompanied by a repeated sequence of notes on a xylophone. The puppet audience clap. Some of them stand up. The puppeteers are in trouble. Some of the puppet threads are tangled. The curtain comes down.

A general clatter comes from behind the theatre, the puppeteers are preparing for the start of their show.

★   ★   ★

A hand lays a card on the table. A man leaves.

There is a brick wall topped by shards of glass, covered in tatters of old posters, now illegible, the silhouettes of cranes, the occasional gull bobbing up above the horizon of the wall before dropping down, the drizzle is turning to mist. These elements fade in and out of visibility depending on the level of light and the density of mist.

An awning protects drinkers sitting on the street outside a bar from drizzle but not from the cold. The drizzle is reaching the level of dispersion at which it becomes mist.

You sit down on an empty chair. The seating is arranged in a semi-circle around the table. The bar behind you has an open window through which the barman passes the beer. Opposite the bar is a high brick wall with shards from broken bottles set into concrete at the top. Above the wall you can see a few of the cranes that were once used to unload the barges or cargo ships.

A man stands up. Lays down his last card and leaves.

Six people are seated around a plastic table placed in front of a bar, they are drinking beer and playing cards. They have oil stains on their hands. The bar is the only thing lit up apart from the occasional streetlamp. Most of the houses have been abandoned. The shipyard is no longer operating.

Far off there is a strange sound. It is difficult to distinguish it from other noises. The sea, a gull, pouring gravel, the creaking cranes, the sound of dogs barking, the traffic, an electric storm. It could be the reverberation of bells, where each tone has lost its distinct shape and merges imperceptibly with the others. A single extended note as if coming from the some eldritch dimension unknown to man, not a human sound, but a slow shattering echo without beginning or end. You don't know when this ricochet effect kicked in, and I suspect you'll be dead before it ends. The dim hush is pornographic, its obscenity lies in the fact that it can't be visualised.

Gulls swoop and glide low over the estuary, catch a pocket of air and are lifted up again to hover and wait before swooping again, they are paler than the sky, their black eyes watching the blank surface of the water. Waiting for the surface to break and then swooping.

One of the cranes is moving. It is a dark shadow against the sky now scarcely lighter. Gleams of light pick out parts of the drizzle. The intermittent creaking sound you hear might be a crane or strange shifts in the air itself.

You walk towards the stray. The dog looks up and fixes you with an unblinking stare. As you move closer, it remains entirely still, unblinking. It could be stuffed. But then, it looked up, turns its head away, and continues cleaning its paws.

A stray dog looms up in the darkness. Its grey pelt resembles the grey of the brick, the grey concrete, the grey sky. It stops in front of you, oblivious of your presence, and starts to clean its paws.

It starts to drizzle. You passed the last store some time ago. The sky suddenly darkens, though far off there is a pale yellowish glow that might be the fading sun or the light from a shipyard. You can see cranes creaking and although muffled by the drizzle, you think you can hear the sound of gravel being poured into shipping containers. Simultaneously the darkness envelops you in an obscene silence, where isolated sounds reach you as if from a long dead world.

You want to follow the estuary down to sea wall, but it's still some way off and you are tired. There are shops selling bread and canned vegetables and beer. Sometimes there's a place to sit and drink coffee, but your stomach refuses to hold down anything stronger than water.

You walk along the canal and down to the estuary. The sky is leaden, despite a strange glow that emanates from the clouds. Colours out of space. The light and your movement have a calming effect, but when you stop and rest you are overwhelmed by feelings of existential dread and can't bear to look at the water.

You leave the flat to get some air. You have felt unsettled since waking up. Your nerves are frayed. Your stomach aches and the pain is spreading through your limbs. The pounding of your blood sends tremors through your body. You have developed an allergy to alcohol.

On the street a group assembles. They are standing in a semi-circle. Is it a queue, or something more sinister? Bon-Euclidean geometries. Voices green, purple and red. Strange folds in the fabric of time and space. The universe buckled, bent and went into reverse. Apocalypse postponed, time running backwards and in slow-mo.

For a while the discussion went well. Most of the group considered it productive. Then a sense of semantic confusion set in, with the opposed factions taking the same terms to mean quite different things. And as for the majority of the collective who in their abstract emptiness stood in so well for that spongy referent "the masses", they grew ever more silent and ever more recalcitrant. The slow drift of ice flows. The dim hush of pornography. The cruelty of deep space.

The town centre is run down. One or two shops appear promising, but they stock the same junk as everywhere else. After an hour you have only made two purchases and you need to stock up on supplies.

The puppets are strewn over the stage, threads hanging limply over them. A long mournful chord comes from the keyboard as the theatre is plunged into darkness. Then the lights come up and the puppeteers move to the front of the stage to bow and bask in the applause.

Debris from the dismantled floor rolled up in a carpet. The materials for a new floor block the door. Reconstruction work cannot begin until the room is cleared.

Stones from the beach were set in the wet concrete. The floor was laid in sections. Each part is slightly different from those that preceded it. A uniform surface could only be created by starting again from scratch.

The floor of the hut is made of stones brought up from the beach. It is easy to trip on the uneven surface.

You go for a stroll. The rocks are green and slippery. As you walk, you brush against their damp surfaces. You take off your shoes and feel brown mud oozing between your toes. A hundred meters from the resort is a hut. Its greenish hue matches the rocks, the stone of the cliff face, the brown and green mud.

The ocean is a neutral grey. The sky is a few shades lighter. Some children are trying to pull a log out of the sea.

You are late. The collective sits around a pale pink table in a room with wall-to-wall carpeting. They were waiting for you to arrive before beginning the meeting, but you assumed they were running late.

She doesn't speak. You are surprised she doesn't want to talk about the row at the puppet theatre. The dim hush is pornographic, its obscenity lies in the fact that it can't be visualised.

You drive slowly. You can only see a few feet beyond the car in the gluey fog. A child was killed on this road, its ghost allegedly appears at night seeking out hit and run drivers.

You pick her up in your car. The windscreen is cracked from a stone that some teenagers threw from a motorway bridge. The windscreen wipers are faulty and it is raining. Behold a pale horse.

★   ★   ★

The use of direct speech is avoided. The children refused to write dialogue. Speech is suggested by the use of music – which implies the tone rather than the sense of these silent exchanges. There are a number of scenes where the gestures of the puppets, the mise-en-scene and the musical accompaniment prove insufficient to generate any definite meaning. At these points the puppets in their opaque nothingness literally become "the ill-will of the people", the spongy referent that animates all post-democratic societies. The cold of interstellar space thousands of degrees below freezing.

Behind the puppet theatre, and to one side, three children provide musical accompaniment. The tallest plays a keyboard, the smallest the triangle, and the third a xylophone.

The stage is a raised platform with a proscenium arch and a real curtain. The backdrop is a large mirror reflecting the faces of the puppet audience, and the real audience behind. Most of the action takes place on the stage within the stage until the roof collapses over the auditorium, then the main drama switches to the audience, with the actors on stage becoming the spectators. The brutality of this violent scene serves to underscore the mixture of farce and sentimentality which characterise the overall tone of the play.

★   ★   ★

A month later there was a discussion that degenerated into a row. The collective, who were elated by the success they believed was bound to follow on from the publication of their pamphlet, are now at war with each other. The puppets representing the collective are only supposed to be operated in crucial scenes. At the beginning of the play there is a vignette in which the artistic director tries to stand up and climb onto the stage to assault an actor who has fluffed his lines, but she is restrained by puppets representing two male actors.

The sense of elation produced by the publication of the pamphlet lasted for weeks. The collective briefly regained a sense of unity and the recalcitrant majority weren't at all concerned by the ways in which the manifesto misrepresented their activities. The coldness of deep space thousands of degrees below freezing.

Puddles all over the place. Puddles of beer, puddles of greenish water. In the puddles, junk is floating. Cigarettes, plastic cups, and broken bottles. There's a bad smell. The aroma is both chemical and organic.

The pamphlet design is plain and clear, visually you have always favoured bold lines and noble simplicity, so this pleases you. That said you would like to cut much of the text. You'd wanted to make a clear statement but the collective insisted on adding caveats and unneeded clarifications until these dense thickets of rhetoric grew inexorably into an impenetrable jungle of words that overran the entire manifesto. From your point of view what was important was to create an immediate impact; but instead you've ended up mirroring the slow drift of an ice flow, the imperceptible passage of distant galaxies through hyper space. The collective is imploding in a subdued fashion, like a slow motion reversal of an explosion or some other catastrophe.

A company member has a cousin who runs a printing workshop. The booklet will be ready in a week. The collective is pleased with the design. It was one of the few things they could agree upon in recent meetings.

★   ★   ★

You are crossing the suburbs, watching shopping malls pass like spaceships in the night sky, clouds across the moon, shadows at dusk. Love without sound. Here come the fleas.

All the seats are upholstered with the same patterned material. It's a variation on a check, and in this deviation the squares have started to drift away from what Euclid would have considered their proper place. These coverings make you think of dying planets sucked into long dead stars, black dwarfs, white dwarfs, and entropy in deep space.

The tinted windows create the impression that it is evening although it's only early afternoon. Dim lights pierce the darkness, and are refracted by the water trickling down the windowpanes. Space is deep.

Back to the old road with its cracks visible in a steady dim light. Reduced to a single lane where surface disintegration has made the road impassable. The highway is imploding in a subdued fashion, like a slow motion reversal of an explosion or some other catastrophe that drags on forever.

Darkness, light, darkness, light. Darkness.... light.... darkness.... light.... Darkness, light, darkness, light. Darkness. Light. Darkness. Light. Darkness, light, darkness, light. Darkness.... light.... darkness.... light.... Darkness. Light. Darkness. Light. Darkness, light, darkness, light. Darkness.... light.... darkness.... light.... Darkness, light, darkness, light. Darkness. Light. Darkness. Light. Darkness, light, darkness, light. Darkness.... light.... darkness.... light.... Darkness. Light. Darkness. Light.

There is only the faintest variation in the hue that distinguishes the scrub of land stretching out to the horizon from the sky. The motorway is in a poor state of repair and its uneven surface sends jolts through the coach. There are long smooth stretches of road with only intermittent lighting. You are engulfed in shadows, the world around you is pitch black, only the diffuse glow of headlights offer any respite from this gloom; then a lit area before you are plunged back into a dark night of the soul. You imagine yourself to be in free fall; fear and trembling. You look for colours out of space in anticipation of the next lit area.

You use your hands to shade a section of the window and look out.

You are already regretting your decision to make this trip. The recent meetings have been tiresome. There was a major bust up, and now it feels as if you are living in what Thomas Hobbes claimed was the natural state of mankind, a war of all against all.

You pass piles of rubbish. The artistic director of your company worships waste; she claims to be drawing on Bataille's theory of solar economics. If nature abhors a vacuum then it must be a social construction, there is nothing at all in deep space.

You take the bus to a small town by the sea with your colleagues from the puppet theatre. They are not talking. They seem unaware of your presence, their attention is elsewhere. Some are looking out of the side windows, and some are staring straight ahead into space. Blackness. The void. Too many light-years between stars. You imagine yourself to be in suspended animation.

Nature abhors a vacuum; time buckled, bent, reversed but never regained. The group is absorbing all the energy it has generated over the years and neutralising it. The resultant dim hush is pornographic, its obscenity lies in the fact that it can't be visualised.

The motorway is in a poor state of repair and is frequently reduced to one lane by road works. The world is imploding in a subdued fashion, like a slow motion reversal of an explosion or some other catastrophe. The best lack all conviction, the worst are filled with a passionate intensity.

An hour's drive from the city there is a town by the sea. The motorway follows the estuary. You take a bus, passing through the suburbs. Outside it's raining. Though it's only the early afternoon, it is already dark. The lights of shopping malls pierce the blackness engulfing the slow flow of traffic from the city.

The kinder operate the puppets using strings. They stand on a raised platform behind the stage. Not all les enfants operate the puppets at any one time, although those bambini not involved often become impatient and push at the children operating the mannequins, so that they can make use of free dolls. As a result the stage becomes crowded with players and their threads get tangled.

The puppets representing the audience are only supposed to be operated in crucial scenes. At the beginning of the play there is a vignette in which a member of the audience tries to stand up and climb onto the stage (he is restrained by two other members of the audience), and these puppets appear again in the scene where the auditorium roof collapses.

There have been several discussions about the function of the puppet theatre. Its themes are topical but the children who participate in the shows remain unaware of this. The performances always contain scenes of Sadean cruelty. The company believes this provides an outlet for childish fears and it is intended to have a cathartic effect. One of the founders of the company wrote their undergraduate dissertation on Wilhelm Reich, another made a study of Peter Brooke's *Marat/Sade*.

★   ★   ★

You stand up and move to the window. Outside the same greying light filtered by the branches of a tree.

There has been talk about putting a booklet together. It would lay out the issues that have been raised in recent meetings. No longer under the reign of will and representation, the group knows very little about the philosophical sources from which aesthetic theory was constructed and instead approaches the many problems it encounters from the perspective of Freud and diagnosis. A company member has a cousin who runs a printing workshop. The pamphlet would be printed in a short run on paper plates and sold at performances.

Far off there is a strange sound. It is difficult to distinguish it from other noises. The sea, a gull, the sound of dogs barking, the traffic, an electric storm. It could be the reverberation of bells, where each tone has lost its distinct shape and merges imperceptibly with the others. A single extended note as if coming from the some eldritch dimension unknown to man, not a human sound, but a slow shattering echo without beginning or end. You don't know when this ricochet effect kicked in, and I suspect you'll be dead before it ends. The dim hush is pornographic, its obscenity lies in the fact that it can't be visualised.

For some time, you sit staring at your notepad. You look up. Some of the group are now standing at the window, looking out through the panes stained by rain and dirt. The grey sky and the trees beyond. The fading light.

Far off the sound of the sea, a gull.

You try to keep notes, partly as a way of remaining attentive to what is being said, although you feel that the same point is being made again and again. However, there are always slight differences in the way this matter is formulated and minor changes of tone. These variations aren't always evident in your notes. Your written record keeps shifting as you attempt to summarise the same old argument in new ways. You imagine the notes you are making being played in the key of G, and you visualise them as deep space; black with flashes of darker blackness.

Every half hour there's a long drawn out sound, a low droning. You visualise it as being green with purple flashes. It is scarcely audible. Some of the group look up, uncertain as to whether they actually heard anything at all. Dogs bark.

The brown table is moved to the centre of the room. There is the screech of chairs on the floor as they are shifted. A man brings in beer, old cups are cleared away. The meetings take place on a regular basis, but all the company members have other responsibilities, and fixing times to meet always entails compromise. For the silent majority in the group, the outcome of the meeting is a foregone conclusion, and there's little point in further discussion. The founders of the theatre company optimistically believed that its activities and influence would continuously expand. That said the collective is now imploding in a subdued fashion, like a slow motion reversal of an explosion or some other catastrophe. The group is absorbing all the energy it has generated over the years and neutralising it.

There is a pause. Someone stands up and goes to the window

Three speakers dominate the proceedings. Each makes the same point, over and over and over again. A recalcitrant majority remain stubbornly silent. They are not convinced by the fine phrases they keep hearing. Those speaking attempt to second guess the positions of the silent majority, but continually return to the same theme, since they are incapable of formulating an argument that runs counter to their own.

There is a pulsing in your head. You are having difficulty concentrating. You have stopped taking notes. You know further discussion is pointless. You visualise the argument as being red with purple flashes.

The meeting is punctuated by long pauses in which the group scrutinises itself and stares stubbornly at the yellow table. Words from an eighteenth-century novel that started a suicide cult spring into your mind. No longer under the reign of will and representation, the group knows very little about the philosophical sources from which aesthetic theory was constructed and instead approaches the many problems it encounters from the perspective of Freud and diagnosis. Someone is keeping notes. During the pauses, the minute taker looks up to see whether the discussion is going to continue. You stare blankly at him then fix your gaze on the bright red table.

A woman brings coffee. Some old cups are cleared away. These meetings take place on a regular basis. The company is convinced the discussion is drawing to a conclusion, although one faction hasn't grasped where the argument is going. Most of the collective believe everything has already been said but since nature abhors a vacuum, time first buckled, then bent, and has now reversed itself. Living in the shadow of silent majorities and having been born in the 1980s, you make a point of having nothing more to say. The discussion is moribund.

In the middle of the room is a large table. Most of those present are either gazing down at the table they're gathered around or else are staring blankly ahead. Several notebooks lie open on the blue table with pens beside them.

There are puddles of beer on the floor with cigarette butts floating in them. There's the perpetual rain dripping through holes in the ceiling, mixing with the beer. There's a rough wooden structure to one side made from old slats nailed together which resembles a stage.

Far off, you can hear the sea, a gull.

A man is sitting on one of the chairs. His reflection is visible in the window. This surprises you because it is not yet dusk and there is only low level lighting in the room. There are chairs scattered about, and around them plastic cups containing dregs of beer.

There's a table, now placed in the middle of the room with chairs set around it. The chairs are plastic with metal frames. All of a whitish hue, though some slightly lighter, these are newer furnishings bought to replace items that had worn out.

You look up for a moment, then down again at your notebook.

The wall-to-wall carpeting has been patched together in areas where it has worn away. The chairs are plastic with metal frames. Although identical in design, they vary in hue depending on the extent of their exposure to dirt and light. There are windows cut into the walls, but it is hard to see anything in the darkness outside despite the low-level lighting in the room.

The discussion is drifting despite the urgent necessity for a collective decision. There are two factions and each is too entrenched to reach an agreement.

Puddles all over the place. Puddles of beer, puddles of greenish water. In the puddles, junk is floating. Cigarettes, plastic cups, and broken bottles. There's a bad smell. The aroma is both chemical and organic.

The company stages plays in schools and public halls. Before each performance, the local area is fly-posted to publicise the event.

The scenery is often adapted from photographs cut out of newspapers. Blown up photocopies, painted backdrops and three dimensional reconstructions have all been used.

Performances are developed collaboratively through improvisation. They are usually based on news events that are of interest to the local community. This process has never been explicitly discussed, but the procedure is so well established that it would be difficult to change it.

★   ★   ★

On the beach a group of teenagers are trying to dismantle a car that was dumped there. The sea is greasy. The shore is covered in large rocks and stones.

You sit down at a table and clear a space amongst the debris of plastic cups. You sip coffee and ponder whether or not to tip the waitress who brought it to you.

Apart from you, there's only one other customer sitting at the bar. The waitress is standing silently beside him. Behind the bar is a large mirror, which reflects the sea through the open window. A gull hovers in the sky.

You turn and go into the café. There are puddles of beer on the floor with cigarette butts floating in them. There's the perpetual rain dripping through holes in the ceiling, mixing with the beer. There's a rough wooden structure to one side made from old slats nailed together resembling a stage.

Streets piled with rubbish. Streets within streets.

Trees, dripping wet, emerge from the greyness.

You catch a glimpse of your face in a shop window and are surprised by the blankness of your expression.

You go back to the café you just passed. You buy a coffee to go and sit in the square, despite the drizzle. On the raised area, two teenagers are having a mock fight, which is turning nasty.

The pulsing in your head is now more regular than when the migraine came on. You find this reassuring.

You walk on and reach an estuary. You have forgotten why you came here.

You make your way past rubbish that is turning to mush in the rain.

You see a group gathered in a bus stop behind you. One of them is pointing, but you cannot see where.

You stop and look into a shop window. The shop is empty and all the displays have been removed. Behind the display case is a mirror. You catch a glimpse of your reflection.

You want to sit down. You follow the man walking purposefully down the street. You find yourself in a neighbourhood whose sidewalks thrum with pedestrians. A market square. In the middle, there's a raised platform where some teenagers are sitting. The shops are mostly closed. In a roofed arcade to one side there is a store selling coffee. You stand at the counter drinking coffee from a plastic cup.

Rubbish is turning to mush in the rain.

It's raining and you have a long trek ahead of you. Stopping at an internet café to check your email you feel the first twinges of a migraine. You know you shouldn't be drinking coffee but instead of wasting the beverage you take an aspirin with it. The combination of coffee and medicine tastes unpleasant. The internet café is cramped. You don't have any email, and this leaves you feeling deflated. You want to go home and get into bed. You can use the migraine as an excuse.

★　★　★

No one has bothered to keep track of the newspaper articles that served as the starting point for the performances. Some of the scripts have been preserved, but these largely consist of instructions to the puppeteers, and it's not always easy to reconstruct the narrative.

The puppet theatre consists of a miniature stage and auditorium. Due of the limited scale of the production, the audience is represented by six puppets sitting with their backs to the real audience.

The string puppets are only capable of rudimentary movements. The theatre is dismantled after each performance. It is stored alongside the puppets in a room at the back of the theatre. Props belonging to various theatres companies are stored together and can be assembled in various combinations to meet the specific requirements of each performance.

A crowd has assembled around the accident.

One passenger was thrown some distance by the impact.

The coast is covered in stones. A group has gathered around a car that crossed the barrier and crashed down onto the rocky shore below.

There's an old wooden structure made from slats. Off-cuts and pieces dismantled from the main structure of the building. The building is slowly collapsing and a new structure is emerging from within. We pay you to play. Even if you have no erection problems! Enlarge your penis with our magic pills! It's as easy as 1, 2, 3!

There's wall-to-wall carpeting, which has been patched together in areas where it has worn away. The furniture is mostly plastic with metal frames, bought in stages to replace items that were worn out. There are windows cut into the walls, but it is hard to see anything in the gloom beyond the window despite the low-level of lighting in the room.

Arranged in front of the puppet theatre are several rows of chairs. Plastic seats and backs with a metal frame. The same whitish hue, though some slightly brighter than others, newer furniture bought to replace items that had worn out.

To one side a wooden structure is covered in newspapers and magazines, books and pamphlets. The drip-drip of the rain outside, audible rather than visible, hidden by a blind pinned over the window. On the wooden structure, among the stacks of booklets, is a puppet theatre made of old off-cuts from an earlier puppet theatre. The puppet theatre is still under construction.

A man a standing among piles of booklets. In another place, the piles have become mounds. The stacks create a warren of streets in the workshop.

Elsewhere there are similar rooms, and yet others identical to it. Newspaper covers the window. A table is set up for a game of cards.

An eye constructs forms in the ebbing darkness. A table with a mirror leaning on it, the mattress on the floor. A patch of light now illuminating a pale hand and wrist. An arm, only vaguely suggested against the paler shade of the blanket. The occasional billowing of the sheet pinned in front of the open window.

The rest of the room is in darkness, a kind of diffuseness in which forms suggest themselves, and then withdraw. The gleam of a mirror, objects scattered over the table, the mattress on the floor, the sleeping body, the faintest stirring of breath, and occasionally minor body movements, mild disturbance in the calm of sleep.

There is a faint stirring, breath is exhaled, then inhaled and exhaled again. The body is shifting under the blankets, almost imperceptibly with the movement being audible rather than visible.

The window is open just a crack. A blind made from a sheet pinned to the window frame billows, and as it does so a rectangle of light expands and contracts, illuminating an arm, a shoulder, a head.

A hand brushes over the covers, the arm follows, both settle in a hollow just beneath the mound of the body. The head shifts into the patch of light. A makeshift blind billows. The light illuminates her head, which is turned towards him, her face obscured by hair.

The distant hum of traffic sounds like waves breaking on a beach.

A patch of light falls across a shoulder. The arm joined to this shoulder is still. The dome of the upper torso emerges from a general softening of detail. The rest of the body is hidden. Faint movement, a tremor of light. The arm shifts followed by the mass of the body. Posture readjusted during sleep.

On the floor to one side, slightly out from the wall, is a mattress. There is a window behind, and a large mirror beside this portal. The window is covered with an improvised blind.

Despite the general greyness, there are noticeable shifts in the clouds. They move in circles as the wind constantly changes direction. This reminds you of grease smeared on a window with a cloth.

One side of the platform is wedged into the cliff, the other three sides are closed off by an iron railing. At the centre is the monument. Or what is described as a monument. Nobody knows what it represents. The monument is a series of abstract forms. It consists of three large concrete triangles of differing widths and heights and angles. A man is standing among these triangles, but only his shoulders and head – which is turned to one side – are visible. He is looking out to sea.

The monument is placed on a concrete platform projecting from the cliff, supported by two iron stilts below. It is reached by descending a series of steps from the top and these are cut into the rock itself. The monument is invisible from the cliff top, and scarcely visible from the beach, where the resort is situated. The main vantage point is from out at sea. It is viewed to best advantage from passing ships.

The sound of waves below, occasionally a gull bobbing up fixing the scene with a motionless black eye, then dropping down again.

Dark shapes float on the surface of the water like photographic paper in a developing tray.

*   *   *

The grey sea endlessly sends small waves up the shore, only to draw them back again.

A crab stirs and attempts to find the sea. It raises its pincers as a hand comes down and picks it up.

The light is dimming. It's a regional effect. The light dims after lunch, then gets steadily brighter into the evening, at which point it gets dark quite suddenly like an electric bulb being switched off.

The door to one of the rooms is propped open. The carpet has been pulled up, and half rolled in the corner, revealing the concrete floor. A table has been set in the middle. It is covered with a paper tablecloth. Around the table are plastic chairs. The table almost fills the room.

The resort isn't large. Perhaps it is only its isolated position that makes it seem like a resort rather than a family hotel. That and its sprawling lay-out.

From this distance, you can scarcely see the movement of the waves. A gull glides at the same height as the cliff top, and then freezes, before dropping into the sea like a stone.

Among the rocks a crab is trying to make its way back to the sea. It seems uncertain of the direction, constantly readjusting its trajectory, pausing repeatedly to gain its bearings.

Between the main building and the sea there's a small pool. An attempt has been made to remove some of the paint, which was flaking badly, and it has been repainted in some places, though each time in a different shade of blue.

The basic structure is made of concrete, which is now badly cracked, and this conjoined with a lack of capital to rebuild it from the foundations up, is the reason the project was abandoned.

The panelling in the foyer has been removed, exposing the plumbing and most of the cabling. Some of the plumbing has been redirected with improvised supports made up of leftovers from the panelling.

Most of the rooms are empty. Much of the furniture has been scrapped or thrown into the sea.

A man stops briefly to look at the horizon. A dog stands alert as if something might suddenly emerge from the sea; a vast shadowy form pushing out of the gelatinous surface, before plunging back down, leaving a succession of concentric circles to bear witness to the event.

Not many people come to the resort. When the building work was abandoned, the connecting road was left uncompleted. The town is a few miles up the coast, and here there is only the resort. Occasionally teenagers descend on it bent on petty vandalism, but there are plenty of other distractions along the coast.

A man is walking along the shore, dragging his feet, a dog circles around him, occasionally darting off to pull something out of the sea. The man forms a silhouette against the dimming light.

There's an inner central courtyard, but where there was once a small pond, there is a hole through which one can see the collapsed masonry on the floor below.

A gull hangs in the air while space shifts around it, an infinitely slow flow of phenomena swirl around the black spot of the gull's eye. The sea's surface, like gelatine, almost still, then breaking into a froth as it reaches the shore. A gull glides steadily, then stops short before dropping like a stone into the water.

The resort is not finished. There's a raised concrete area for an extension. It must have been set a while ago because it has already started to crack. In its current state, it resembles a stage. In some areas beach stones were pressed into the concrete when it was still wet. It's not clear if this was part of a plan that was later abandoned, or an intervention by a passer-by.

There are moments when the light changes, though without the impression of a gradual shift to new weather conditions, as if the fresh atmospheric situation had arrived instantly and yet the transition takes place without a cut or a jolt. One simply accepts that there has been a transformation.

It's neither warm nor cold. There is a roof of grey cloud that is almost still, made of an infinitely soft substance that will never break.

The rain isn't cleansing but instead covers everything with a gelatinous skin.

When the park was laid out in the eighteenth-century you could gaze over the trees, across the town and down to the sea. The trees, which once framed the view, now obscure it. Their slow growth was like curtains rising very slowly at the beginning of a matinee. Now the trees themselves are the sole performers, bowing slightly in the breeze. The raised platform has become the stage and is no longer the auditorium, and the trees are the audience, and a man standing on it, slowly sinking into his coat, is a solitary actor.

Seated to one side, a man looks down at his watch and then up at the trees obscuring the view. He isn't comfortable on the rustic seating, and is steadily sinking into his coat as he attempts to stay warm.

Rain drips through the holes in the roof of the seating area on the viewing platform.

The viewing platform is covered with weeds. The concrete is cracked, ill suited to the damp climate and the harsh winter. The base is a raised semi-circle of concrete set into the slope of the hill with steps up one side. A semi-circular seating arrangement mirrors the curve of the base but with a smaller diameter. The seating is sheltered from behind and above by a wooden structure. The benches are constructed from iron and wood. The ironwork imitates the branches of a tree.

Among the dripping trees and barely sheltered by rain streaked leaves, a man is sitting, his head bowed down as he attempts to keep warm.

Fifty feet away is a hidden viewing platform. The design of the park makes the terrain difficult to navigate. There isn't a path to the viewing platform, and you are forced to switch direction in areas that are overgrown. The viewing platform is set into the side of the hill, and is easy to miss.

★　★　★

To one side is a stage lit by two spot lights. The rest is darkness.

★　★　★

A small crowd gathers. Though barely acknowledging each other, barely lifting their heads, they are all members of an experimental theatre company who are engaged in a pre-arranged street performance.

Cracked panes, with a mirror behind, now reflecting a group gathered in the bus shelter. They are drinking beer and don't appear to be waiting for a bus.

To one side is a bus shelter, where a man is drinking beer. He is watching the teenagers on the raised area at the centre of the market place.

The buildings around the square are older than the plinth and have been maintained in a better state of repair. It was constructed to replace a fountain, but now acts as a raised area where teenagers can sit and bait each other as they smoke.

The base was originally intended as a plinth for a statue that was never erected. The unexpected success of the opposition party in a council election resulted in the politically sensitive bronze being melted down after it was sold as scrap metal.

There's a raised platform that was once the base of an ornamental fountain, this water feature has been removed. Teenagers are sitting on it and sparking up.

Towards the back of the arcade is a store with a counter running the full length of the façade, it sells coffee. Across from the store is an empty shop. The window is cracked and dirty. Through it an empty display shelf is visible. Behind the shelf is a large mirror, and in it is a reflection of a group of teenagers sitting smoking on the plinth at the centre of the square.

The buildings intended to serve as retail outlets are mostly empty. Their windows gleam blankly.

The square is enclosed by buildings. At the centre is a raised plinth that once supported a fountain. To one side is a small arcade of shops.

Puddles all over the place. Puddles of beer, puddles of green-ish water. In the puddles, junk is floating. Cigarettes, plastic cups, and broken bottles. There's a bad smell. The aroma is both chemical and organic.

Water reflecting the bare branches of trees planted intermittent-ly through the square, a grey roof of clouds behind.

At the centre is a raised platform. The base for a statue that has not been erected. The concrete is cracked, the rain trickles through these crevices. Around the raised platform, the square is peppered with puddles. There's a strange smell – the aroma is both chemical and organic.

Paint flaking from walls covered in announcements for events long since passed. To one side a table with a flimsy box-like structure made from old cut offs. Towards the back, a large mir-ror partly reflecting the room and the windows, and a number of chairs arranged in front, still empty, though a figure can be seen in the door at the back of the room.

No other vehicles. The motorway now reduced to two single lanes and the approaching glow of the boarder post, which inter-rupts the seemingly endless sweep of the road.

Then back to the old road with visible cracks and a steady dim light, reduced to a single lane in places where the cracks have made parts of this highway impassable.

The illuminated areas scarcely more penetrable, they represent no more than a change of hue.

Only the faintest variation of hue distinguishes the scrub of land stretching out to the horizon from the sky. It is a long time since the motorway was properly repaired, its uneven surface sends jolts through the coach. A long stretch that has been resurfaced is only intermittently lit. Deep passages engulfed in darkness, almost black, scarcely guided by the diffuse glow of the headlights, then a lit area, the darkness transformed from black to grey, then you are engulfed by the gloom again, which is somehow out of space, a sense of free-fall, awaiting the next lit area.

Two hands shade a section of the window, a face pressed against the pane, looking out.

No one speaks. The passengers are either looking out of the window, or staring blankly ahead. A series of reflections, and reflections of reflections, despite the low level lighting in the bus. All this superimposed over the passing landscape.

Shadowy forms pass behind the pointilism of raindrops, dark drifts beneath ripples of water.

Lights from malls are refracted in the rain streaked windows. Distant shadows in the dimming light. The passing traffic sounds like breaking waves. Lines of traffic drawn back, then swelling forward and rushing past. The slow staccato of traffic jars against the gentle drift of distant buildings.

There is little traffic. What there is appears initially as a diffuse glow pushing out of this substance that isn't quite darkness. The lighted areas shroud space instead of revealing it.

Piles of debris emerge from the greyness.

The road, scarcely visible, is a series of nebulous veils repeatedly penetrated by the headlights of the bus.

There is a cracked pane where some teenagers threw a stone from a motorway bridge. The windscreen wipers malfunction. The bus is in semi-darkness, the passengers are silent.

The driver looks in his rear view mirror. The coach is occasionally lit up by street lamps, and then plunged into darkness, then light, then darkness again. Some of the passengers are looking out of a window, others are simply staring ahead.

The road is covered in cracks. Some parts have been sealed off. The highway is being dismantled. Some areas are lit, some not, though this bears no relation to the road works. Sometimes it's possible to count fifty, sixty seconds of darkness, then light, then gloom again, the headlights scarcely providing any radiance, creating instead something closer to a diffuse veil constantly penetrated by the beams of the bus. Then another lit area where the cracks become visible again, the debris of the road works, piled in mounds. Then gloom.

She appears to be looking directly at you, though there's no way she can see you. Nevertheless, there are certain signs that could make her aware of your presence. Her face is lit eerily by a mirror reflecting a beam of light coming through a crack in the ceiling. The rest of her body is in shadow. She continues to stare towards you, but after a while you suspect that she's sleeping with her eyes open, in some sort of trance.

There are puddles of beer on the floor with cigarette butts floating in them. Rain is dripping through holes in the ceiling, mixing with the beer. There is a rough wooden structure to one side which is made from old slats nailed together and resembles a stage.

There's wall-to-wall carpeting, which has been patched together in areas where it has worn away. The furniture is mostly plastic with metal frames. There are windows cut into the walls but it is hard to see anything in the darkness outside despite the low-level lighting in the room.

Behind the stage area the wall is lined with mirrors. The room was used as a dance studio before being rebuilt. One of the mirrors is cracked and reflects the room in altering perspectives. Also reflected in this mirror are seven people sitting on plastic chairs.

A semicircle of chairs is arranged in front of a structure that was once a stage, but which is now covered with piles of old newspapers and magazines. The stage floor has collapsed in the middle and old newsprint spills into it. A man is sitting in one of the chairs and his reflection fills one of the windows.

A man sitting on one of the chairs is reflected in a window. It is not yet dusk and so you are surprised to see such a sharp reflection when there is only low-level lighting on in the room. There are chairs scattered about, and around them plastic cups containing dregs of beer.

To one side there's a rickety structure that may have been the stage, with chairs scattered around it. Seven chairs have been arranged in a semicircle. They have a plastic seat and back which is supported by a metal frame. They are all of same whitish hue, although some are slightly brighter, they are newer pieces of furniture bought to replace items that had worn out.

The mechanism is complex. There's a system of mirrors producing a series of reflections. Both the stage and the mirrors revolve through a number of orbits, so that it is impossible to know whether you are looking directly at the event on the stage or at a reflection, or even a reflection of a reflection.

Nowhere for the gaze to settle. Everything crushed or torn open. Wounds within wounds. Coldness and cruelty.

Vermin swarmed through the rubble picking at human flesh. Entrails strewn amid blocks of concrete and shattered glass. Dead meat oozing with blood scattered throughout and beyond the wrecked theatre of the world.

Severed limbs were thrown beyond the building, where they were consumed by rats and stray dogs.

Parts of bodies, hands, and feet were crushed under the rubble. Her neck was severed by a metal girder, which knocked the head two metres from her chest.

Scattered body parts. Blood oozed over the rubble. Bodies sliced up by falling glass and crushed by tumbling masonry. Eyes pierced by rusty nails jutting from broken sections of the building's wooden frame.

The ceiling of the theatre collapsed during a performance. Masonry tumbled onto the stage, and the stage machinery collapsed too.

The stage is a raised structure lit by two spot lights. Beyond it there are seven rows of chairs. Behind the stage there is a wall lined with mirrors. There is no other scenery. The chairs that seat spectators during performances are reflected in the mirrors.

MORE EXPERIMENTAL NOVELS VIA THE LEDATAPE ORGANISATION

Neil Palmer
EXECUTIVE SUFFICIENCY

2010, 5½ x 8½ in., 120pp

In the uptight world of the London media elite, even the opening of a new exhibition of Prison Art is regarded as an exciting adventure. Senses dulled and out of his depth in the face of an unfolding story of the real elite, Bryn Nolan rouses himself from his cocoon of self-confidence and rises to a challenge that only he, London's premier public relations operator, can overcome. The wild valleys and mountains of the Caucasus and the even wilder alleys and concrete rifts of the London landscape collide in this meticulously researched novel of high adventure happening elsewhere to other people.

Neil Palmer
PLACE EXPLOSION

2010,5½ x 8½ in., 136pp

From Magic Localism to post-regionalist eco-apocalypse realism, from materialist anti-irrationality to the livin' end of punk rock mythology, from collective identities to utter individualism, from alienation to belonging, from Cambridge Royal Mail sorting office to Hove public library, the stories collected together in *Place Explosion* describe the fistula between knowledge and consciousness that has emerged in this totally precedented era of total control.

Place Explosion delves deep into the unlucky dip of popular culture in the long late-20th century.

Shane Jesse Christmass
ACID SHOTTAS

2013, 5½ x 8½ in, 234pp

The purveyors of consciousness expanding LIED! They told you to TUNE IN, TURN ON, DROP OUT - but they did not qualify this statement. Dropping out from what to where to what again. Dropping from sanity to madness, to bad breath, the horrible cheap tab. ACID SHOTTAS is the aftermath. It is the mid-80s. Heavy Metal is rife. It's pre-MDMA. Tacky, inexpensive acid is on the streets. This is the decade of hate. Cold War. Reaganomics. This is the aftermath. Wolf-shot words written to Dancehall and Acid House. This is Vietnam....

Aaron Goldberg
FOUTRE LA MERDE, DANS

2011, 5 x 7 in., 120pp

Multi award-winning novelist Aaron Goldberg returns with his debut award-winning novel *Foutre la merde, dans*. A recipient of a $400,000 Arts Grant from Merdeoch University, *Foutre la merde, dans* is a by-the-dots piece of contemporary literature, exploring notions of identity, sexuality, multi-multiculturalism, oppression from the dominant paradigm, persecution, depression, repression, acceptance and the ultimate triumph of getting your own retrospective at the Wheeler Dealer Centre, as well as increasing your Facebook friend count and your industry currency by 100,000 points/friends.

OUR SHIT BEATS THEIR GOLD

www.ingramcontent.com/pod-product-compliance
Lightning Source LLC
Chambersburg PA
CBHW031838170626
46807CB00004B/1514